DETROIT PUBLIC LIBRARY

3 5674 00771631 0

G1 STACKS

DETROIT PUBLIC LIBRARY

BROWSING LIBRARY
5201 Woodward
Detroit. MI 48202

DATE DUE

NEVER DIE

BARRY HANNAH

NEVER DIE

HOUGHTON MIFFLIN / SEYMOUR LAWRENCE

Boston 1991

c.1

Copyright © 1991 by Barry Hannah
All rights reserved

For information about permission to reproduce selections from
this book, write to Permissions, Houghton Mifflin Company,
2 Park Street, Boston, Massachusetts 02108.

Library of Congress Cataloging-in-Publication Data

Hannah, Barry.
Never die / Barry Hannah.
p.   cm.
ISBN 0-395-51560-2
I. Title.
PS3558.A476N48   1991   91-293
813'.54 — dc20   CIP

Printed in the United States of America

BP 10 9 8 7 6 5 4 3 2 1

BLBL.
AUG 22 1991

For Sam Lawrence
and my children, Po, Teddy, and Lee

NEVER DIE

In a 1910 frontier town rife with corruption, a dwarf and a judge who own the town and the judge's daughter take part in a dark comedy of lust and revenge.

Back during the Civil War Kyle Nitburg was just twelve years old. The war was going badly around New Orleans, where he and his poor but beautiful mother lived. His father had gone off to fight in Virginia, near Richmond, they thought, but there was no communication and barely any chicken and peas. There might as well have been no father and barely any world.

Some ragged-looking people on horses came through the yard repeatedly and his mother would get on the back of a horse and ride off with them. Then some sheets of paper fell in the yard off a deep blue rushing cavalry that he knew was the Union.

He knew his mother was a spy. The next morning he ran over the paths to the blue people and turned her in. The reward was one hundred real dollars.

His mother was hanged on a railroad bridge.

1

Kyle Nitburg got the money and stood there with acne on his face, smiling, next to the rail where his mother stood poised on her bare feet before she hung. Somebody took a picture of this scene. An early cameraman got it perfectly in black and white. He was a student of Mathew Brady, the great Civil War photographer.

Later, when Nitburg moved west to escape the infamy, he made enough money to marry Nancy Beech, from an old distinguished but poor family in San Antonio. The marriage did not go well after she delivered herself of a daughter, Nandina, and Kyle Nitburg with his partner, James Ford, of the same stock who would shoot Jesse James in the back for money, rode out to West Texas with her to deal with a Comanche chief called Bad Cloud. They had just the three horses and met fifty Indians. Nitburg sold his wife into slavery as Ford watched, with his nervous hands around his Winchester rifle, sighing with a whining sound throughout this ignominy. He was looking over the plain toward the high mesa where Mexico started.

The Indians sold them a few blankets and soft boots while they bought Nitburg's wife for four thousand dollars in real gold. It was a bright red twilight and Ford wanted to move off. Nitburg wanted to sit there on his horse for a while.

One member of the Indians wasn't an Indian. He was a white photographer. He took a picture of Nitburg selling his wife and Ford, restless, trying to go home, wherever it might be.

Ten years later Nitburg had read the law thoroughly like a rabbi with a magnifying glass. His ally Ford had been shot in a saloon in Austin just for being a backbiting pest with high pretensions. He'd limped away with his penis shot off. But he had never much needed it anyway, and sailed to New York to nurse his real wounds.

Nitburg became a judge in a beige waste spot with the name of Dolores Springs. He married the blind millionaire widow Charlotte Dunning, whose son lived just fifty miles away, some rods down the road, as they said then. He was big and loved his mama. He would bop you on the snout quick if you mistreated the blind woman. Her full name was Charlotte Agnes Dunning. Nandina, who had become the local schoolteacher, sometimes called her Hagness. The old woman wore her hair to the floor and adored it.

Navy Remington, a sea captain who had known Nitburg in New Orleans after the war, settled in with the bounty of his old age at a sheep ranch forty miles east of the town now called Nitburg. He was an old bachelor with his memories, growing deafer and deafer, eventually buying a yellow automobile, a Winton Flyer. Nitburg continued to cheat, lie and steal, and pretty soon the town and much land around it was his.

The nephew of Navy Remington called himself Fernando Muré. He had a university education and was a gunfighter almost without intending to be. He had killed three men with his silver pistols in

3

Dallas. He played the game of seven-up and was a mediocre gambler, but that afternoon he won a fortune from three angry men with shotguns loaded for doves. They backed away from the table and when Fernando sensed what was happening he threw over the table, got behind it and received fire. With his left hand around his groin he ducked his head and fired through the table itself, took out the other pistol and did the same. When the smoke cleared, the table was shredded, but he had not suffered a scratch. All three of his adversaries lay dead.

★

— 'Member that good-looking lady had that German shepherd?
   — Yeah?
   — Hmmm, hmmm, heh heh.
   — What . . .
   — The woman with the dog?
   — Yeah.
   — Hyun hyun yhunuch.
   — Aw persist, Nitburger.
   — Hyun hyun.
   — My God. My God.
Neb Lewton and his deputy were talking. Lewton had killed a man thirty years ago. Lewton was the sheriff, along with his twin brother, Dantly. But he was old now, with cobwebs between his thumb and trigger finger, rust flaking out of his rectum. Leaves it there on the chair seat when he departs some-

where like to the other chair four and a half feet away where he scooches off, right now.

But Neb has dreams — hard physical things — those beasts, those mad hoydens, their quick feet in the gutter. He just pursues the old nastiness in his memories. He curses the light. He curses God. The world is really ugly and the people are sad, he thinks. Tom the Negro plays your favorite tune for a quarter. In his mind he goes back to that Mexican woman with hair on her arms. He still has a prodigious want for harlots. He knows he is crooked and fat and old, a daft old poisonous person, but something still calls him from a cool garden in his memory. Woman's voice with evil on her tongue. He is near rage every minute. I hate this town Nitburg, he thinks. I'm just a pitiful old creature who can't do a thing about it. He dreams of dead women underwater. They had brilliant futures, but now they were just slabs of flesh underwater. It gave Neb Lewton pleasure.

★

Fernando had his fedora and his long tan Mexican cigarettes, but he was worried. He was a creature of perfect idleness but he had projections about his coffin factory and, mainly, the way to buy one of the new motorcycles he had seen in New Orleans just recently. He had promised very loudly the other night that he would burn this town and he still meant to. It was bad enough, but now the Chinese had moved in and he had no use for the

5

race. He was thirty-eight years old and had the one constant girlfriend, Stella, a slut with tuberculosis. He had his friends at the pool hall and credit all over town. He was fine amigo with the preacher. Bankrupt almost, Fernando considered a lengthy suicide. That is, an extended debauch of fine wines until his speech slurred and he died in a fury of drums and small-caliber gossip.

But no, for he was merely thirty-eight and it would take too great a dedication. Again he delivered himself to the task at hand, which was a race through nullity and mere style. On third thought, he was tired, and humiliated. On fourth, he was a young man who had sworn to burn the town, which was mainly wooden. The town of Nitburg had rumors of Fernando's decline.

Fernando with his Mexican matches and his scarves and the small gelding he rode. His dancing testicles named Juan and Manuel. He was making progress through the *diem* quite finely. Nobody had been killed lately and the women were blossoming around him. Consider Nandina Nitburg with her curly long black hair. Consider the constant Stella, and his own singing voice, an exquisite instrument of wind and esophagus. But Stella was sick to the point of vomiting every other moment, though he attended to her with his handsome and devilish humor.

I must see everybody, I must do everything, he thought.

I must remember to buy or borrow some bullets.

I must stop becoming a totally newborn asshole every day.

I must make my mark on the dry soil; must live to say hello again without ugly thought or criticism. The bitterness is wearing me down, making me frown in my sleep, making my tits wilt and things of that nature. He was so sad he was turning androgynous.

Women watched, though, while Fernando was thinking this, and wished he would assault them like a shovel of passion pushed in the grave of their lusts.

Vicious tumbleweeds blew near and hit the alleys of the Nitburg Hotel. It was turning dark.

The sky was gray and the two trees on Main Street were rustling. Fernando swayed past the sheriff's office, being drunk. He connived, he wandered artfully beyond the new moon just now in the air. He wore filthy white pants with black stitching all tucked in big elegant cavalry boots. I remand myself to the custody of myself, he thought. He wore his last pistol but there were no bullets in it. Maybe he had gambled them away. My God, I remember when I was alive, he said to himself.

Fernando, soberer, walked down the alley next to the Chinese shelters and was promptly busted over the knee by a dwarf named Edwin Smoot, an associate of Judge Kyle Nitburg. The dwarf hit him on the knee with a baseball bat as hard as he could. Fernando howled and went down, raising a mad dust around his person. Smoot made himself scarce but could not erase the teensy bootprints. They looked exactly like an elf dancing around in flour.

So that night with his great swollen knee Fernando lay on a table in Doc Fingo's office staring up into Fingo's diagnostic eyes, listening for the rustle of little feet on the carpeted parlor above them where he knew the little tapper stayed. Doc Fingo kept his eyes dead on the knee and did not look at Fernando's eyes much at all, while Fernando listened, listened, sharpening his ears, pitying and yet stalking little Smoot, who might be above.

— It truly hurts, I'll say that, said Fernando.

— Certain it does. Most certainly, Mr. Muré.

— Christ of God! howled Fernando. Fingo had just touched the knee, lifting the calf and moving it back and forth, then wobbling the leg sideways.

— The pain, no? asked Fingo.

— Big as a melon and black and green. Yes it hurts, you goddamned fool!

— Easy. I'm the only doc you got. Researching for crackage.

— Holy fuckeroo. Stick some drugs in it, can't you?

— In good time. The kneecap and surrounding is a delicate matter.

— Tell me about it.

Fernando was not listening for little Smoot anymore. His eyes were flying over the vials in the locked glass cabinet, already thirsty for everything

8

there. Presently though not presently enough Doc Fingo neared him with a needle.

— This will give you some ease, said the old physician with almost no ears.

Fernando reached up and grabbed his arm. — And give me another one of those right after this one. Fingo blinked.

— That's a lot of drug. You allergic to anything?

Fernando held the free wrist of Fingo in a terrible grip, until the shot began taking him away. — Edwin Smoot, he giggled, though it mightily pained his kneecap. — And I want everybody who ever crossed me to come in here and kiss my ass, he said.

— Poor boy.

Fingo looked directly at his eyes, satisfied the drug was well in him. Fernando relaxed his grip and his eyes narrowed as in a happy conspiracy.

— You're asking a lot for someone of your . . . eh . . . vocation, said Fingo. He whispered through his short wet beard. — What do you finally want, Muré?

— Burn down the town and see the scum run, yawned Fernando. — I thought Evil was big but it's really a mighty, mighty . . . small thing.

★

Fernando was asleep, or so thought Fingo. He beheld the closed eyes and the easy-rising chest under the black scarf, the round red imprint of the hat still on his sweating head, just beneath the flatted bangs with just now three drops of drug sweat racing down to Fernando's eyebrows and through them down to the eyelids, under which Fernando's big near-black eyes were yet awake, his ears coming back too, sharp for the tread of Edwin Smoot, a relative of Joe Snag, who would have killed Fernando in the alley and not just smashed him in the kneecap had he found himself in the vantage of small Edwin.

Now Fernando heard Smoot creeping down the carpeted stairs, the nick of a small heel on a plank as he missed the carpet by one inch. Fernando was alive behind his closed lids, with Fingo unseen holding the next hypo as if beckoned like a zombie by Fernando's request.

My holy ruler, thought Fingo. I'm in love with the man and my complete little vicious empire is threatened by him, but I adore this fool. Look at his freckles from the sun, his slim muscular leg, and the knife scars. He jammed the hypo in Fernando's thigh. Highly unmedical, he thought. This man needs a kiss.

Fingo sat on the floor spread-legged, despising the morbid fat of his inner thighs. He wanted to join the wrath of Fernando and so rose, waddled, and fixed himself a large shot, as Edwin Smoot eased himself down, in his hipwalk, hand around the floorpost of the baroque stairway.

Smoot wore a very large hat and did not think of himself as small. To himself, he cut a considerable figure: more dangerous, because ignored and ridiculed by drunkards, more special, because given an unwanted blessing by religious women he passed in the streets. There was a secret place for his own virtues and it would never be known to the regular folks. Up there it was ugly and vicious and he was working for himself in a deeper and vaster mileage than for instance the fool Doc Fingo and his mere several thousands. It was not the money, not the height, not the width, not the space or time, idiots, but the *depth*. He was like a great root that barely had a tree above, looking at another region entirely, down in the earth seven feet like a gleaming root, among small, elegant, lusty rootwomen with breasts round and hard-nippled. — Ooma, Ooma, he said, imagining some underground talk for himself.

But Fernando heard his polished little boots mincing toward the room. Doc Fingo had given himself a shot. His tolerance was very low.

Fernando raised the lid of his left eye, not the right, which Smoot would see from his underlingness, advancing nastily for the other knee with a spadelike razor in the dark to the right of Fernando, lying there, still, like a dummy abject on morphine. Fernando had tricks in wait, but what could he see with his left eye only — what was there to grab, what was there to jump up for and say? Worse, as he'd quit financing and courting her, he began hallucinating this gossipy woman from his *right* side, her picture thrown up in the air before him, a troll with her tongue on fire, spewing molten teeth from her mouth. She grew stronger with that right eye shut, and by so much that he couldn't bear it — had to open the eye — and there was the dwarf Edwin Smoot, with a naked chest and gold Saint Christopher medal on it. Lurking, peering at Fernando, he was dressed in black leather rider's pants and infantile black lustrous boots. Fernando had never seen Smoot full in the face before and neither had Smoot Fernando, head to head, first time betwixt opposable eyes.

— Hey, you're not a bad-looking man for late thirties, said Smoot.

Fernando could look but not speak.

— Stoned, thank God, said Smoot, glancing down at the snoring corpus of Doc Fingo. — I could cut your hamstrings, long partner. Then what would you do? My big Fernando. You're bound for catastrophe and too beautiful to die so young. Your speed. Maybe should crack the other knee. Who do you think you are, out in this whispering near-desert?

Fernando was taken by the second injection and could not even murmur by now. His cupped hands lay limp around his peter, a weak basket on the filthy white, dusty cloth of his crotch. Only his painful right knee was alive, and he fell dead asleep from fear of Smoot. Also, he was something of a rotter, a nasty man himself, and he invited the morphine in to forget this. He misted toward further calumnies and beyond into the revenges of the swamp and desert. He was from New Orleans and the water was coming up visibly around his boots, now that he was in the sand and dreaming. He hardly felt it when Smoot cracked his other knee with a baseball bat.

★

Judge Nitburg and his daughter, Nandina, the happy-lapped big spender with center-parted jet black tresses and intensely articulated legs (she had something of the evil eye too), were wrapped up kissing each other's teeth, fond of each other just an elf's step beyond common practice and her more so because of the judge's late rapid wealth.

Then Edwin Smoot knocked at the window, making circles of breath and drawing crosses in them, viewing them.

Judge Nitburg snapped away from Nandina, outraged.

— Can't you use the door like others, you little scrotum?

Nandina raced along a wing off in the back, both hands full of lucre. Her old stepmother was rich and blind and she almost tripped over the ancient thing there in the rocking chair in her long black coat and high-top lace-up granny shoes, gray hair down to the floor, slashing the air with her cane and nicking Nandina a light one on the breast.

— Creature! nagged the old woman.

— Hagness! whispered Nandina, dropping money.

Smoot opened the front door, veered in, and shambled. The waddling nub, thought Nitburg, into his handkerchief. But he is necessary. The judge had sold many a decision from the bench and the dwarf had even once poisoned for him. The judge was the same age as Smoot, and he envied the dwarf's full tangled head of hair, whereas he was bald and only his sideburns were full, colored like speckled sarsaparilla.

— Our business? sought the judge.

— He's ailing with two cracked kneecaps, your worship. Smoot removed his hat and his curls fell out. The dwarf was solemn and the judge could have laughed in his face — for what you could buy with short cash.

Smoot brought his bandana out and wiped the sweat from the moon of his brow. He kept staring flatly and long at Judge Nitburg. He swallowed a gob of anxiety.

— What?

— Hitting a drugged man on the knee . . . takes it out of a fellow. It don't seem rightly . . . humane.

The judge's face expressed nothing, but he was enjoying a black glee in there. Fellow . . . humane . . . indeed, he considered.

— It's done all the time, Smoot. There's a whole continent of kneecrackers south of the border. I guess you've never been there, though.

— No sir. There was the matter of . . . an automobile.

— Oh yes, of course. Would you like a cordial?

The judge raised a tremendous cut-glass decanter, nearly as big as a wastepaper can, and touched two silver tumblers on the linen.

— I wish you'd remember it makes me sick, declared Smoot, though the offer seemed to relax him. — I'll take just ice water.

— I'd have to go get the ice, said the judge.

— The automobile would have to be . . . different, you understand. As for the rest, I prefer mainly stainless all over. Smoot took the plain water.

Prefer, thought the judge, howling joylessly inside. — You want a suit of armor to match?

— For your information, your worship, I'm not even here. Laughter at me don't scratch me one bit anymore.

— Automobiles like that are hard to find. Hard even to *discover*. You'd, eh, be *here* if you had one, wouldn't you?

— In a way, said Smoot.

— You're in south of the border trade and don't even know it, Smoot. Get you some medals and some filigree and those . . . what? . . . shoulder croppings, couple of speeches to make, no freedom of the press. You can borrow my sunglasses. You're not amused?

— Fernando's uncle has an automobile.

— Many, many rods away.

— Not too many. Forty miles. The eastern county.

— What do you expect from Fernando?

— He will go to places slower or have less places to go. I predict he will get back on the whiskey full time and stare at sparrows for an indeterminate period. Will collapse from spite and self-pity. Is

15

what. Doc Fingo could also, with some ingenious-ness . . . evolve a morphine habit in him. I see Mister Muré as an addictive type . . . like you, Your Honor.

— Me? The judge ventured toward outrage, then stepped back. — I can take this stuff or leave it. Set of slight nerves at this point is all I've got.

— Don't mean necessarily the spirits, said Smoot.

The judge glared down at Smoot but would not allow himself a sneer. — I'll work . . . on the auto-mobile. In the meantime, how about combing old wife Agnes's hair? You get tender with that hair, small wheeler, and money falls right out of her ears.

— But, complained Smoot, hat in hands, — it's irksome.

— I've done it myself. Life is *duty* too, you under-stand.

— Yours, your worship. I defer.

★

Nandina, second story of the manse, was now through counting and ready to settle her options: a spell in Navy Remington's auto, a quail hunt on her pony, cards with the three sluts in town, or memo-rizing a Psalm.

> The Lord is my shepherd, I shall not want
> He makes me lie down in green pastures.
> He leads me beside still waters,
> He restores my soul.

16

Even though I walk through the
Valley of the shadow of death,
I fear no evil.
For thou art with me. Thy rod and thy
Staff, they comfort me.

Thou preparest a table before me
In the presence of my enemies.
Thou anointest my head with oil.
My cup overflows.

Surely goodness and mercy shall follow me
All the days of my life.
And I shall dwell in the house of the Lord
Forever.

That's a tidy dream, she thought.

Had the young unmarried preacher in town any prospects, she would throw another, chaster outfit into her trunk. The young preacher, McCorkindale, had once flown in an airplane, but his hand was chilly when she touched it and he was poor as sand. She could hardly imagine him naked, either. Thing was, she saw him on a hill shining, white and hairy with a few listless sheep on the slope below him. Curious he wore the long black coat and the immensely brimmed hat, as if to avoid the light he was sworn to deliver to his flock. Or perhaps it was an aviation coat and he owned no other. Some said he was studying for the law on the side. There was a career, but it seemed a very slow train coming to her. On the other hand, when he leaned in a saloon and drank his whiskey he had a faraway, fetching look . . . the look of . . . a valid aviator with a deed to the sky. His flying mate, "Python" Weems, was good with a bullwhip, but hardly ever in Nitburg.

Oh oh oh Fernando, gosh she wished Pop liked him. He was a contagious man, practically unswervable, though she had not yet made out his direction. What he did for a living was misty, but it had something to do with stealing from the poor and raiding the Indian reservation. He'd dispossessed a family of eleven Chinese from a shack. Hadn't he? These were tales told by Judge Nitburg. Her pop. And it was hard to believe when you saw the charitable twinkle in Fernando's black eyes, or the way he strode down the sidewalk planks, even with a full load of whiskey in him — like a ship's captain without a boat, in nature of his uncle Navy Remington, cavalier, imperial, yes, like in his head he bore a letter from the king.

He was nothing on the guitar, though, and did not ride well on a horse. Said he was waiting for a motorcycle. He was sort of friends with Reverend McCorkindale, wasn't he?

Nandina owned a number of dogs. They ran around her feet like avid geese, even following her into town across the desert. One of them, more songful and blacker than the rest, she named F. Muré. Fernando had learned to write songs in prison. This was a fact. He had a cunning and lonesome voice that touched down to her feet. Perhaps the Reverend was friends with him because he, too, liked the church piano, always better than that lambasted whore they had in the saloon. The canine Muré she would cuddle on her bed for hours. Then she would betray it.

There was a rumor that Fernando might one day have his own saloon and, furthermore, a factory of some sorts. Perhaps. Nandina had heard also that he might call a hiatus on the liquor. Nandina preferred wickedness that showed a profit, his gun hand to her lips, his tongue to her tongue, and no vomiting afterward.

She hoped the judge had got the dwarf to comb Agnes's detestable hair. The old thing would want to play badminton soon, before Nandina left for Nitburg, that was for sure. The judge urged it. The old woman would smile and come forth with any number of dollars. She would flail the racquet back and forth as you hit right into her. If she touched or smacked a birdie, she howled with ecstasy, but you were in for a whole tournament. Finally, she would perspire and fade, and then, get rolled back on her wheelchair, for a nap, most likely sleeping behind her sunglasses already. The volume of the woman was awful. From her blindness she had developed a stronger sense of screaming. "Child! Child! Smote *that* birdie, baby!"

What gruesome charity could really abide her?

The Reverend counted the old woman as one of his flock, and she had rewarded his attention. — In your blindness, Mother Agnes (her son, Robert, was fifty, two counties away; he was large and would beat the punk out of anyone not reverent toward his ma), the Reverend once asked her, — have you found stronger faith? What's it like in there, Mother Agnes? Tell it all.

— Naw. But God sure owes me one, said the woman. — Stroke my feathers, young man.

She held the Reverend's cold, pale, hair-backed hand in both of hers.

At the church she loved the trumpet, the cymbals and the piano foremost, lifting her greedy blind voice through the single stained-glass window. So there was church every Sunday to take her to. They could have an automobile if only the woman believed they existed.

— They do, they do! Nandina remonstrated.

— Can't prove it by me. Think you can trick me with that noise?

— But you've been in one.

— Guileful creature. That could've been anything.

More than almost anything Nandina wanted an automobile. And to be a member of some riding gang, though she was getting a little old for it. She did not sit well; she did not lounge well. She could not brood, meditate, or twit. The wind in her hair, a terrified javelina plunging before her, her heels given to everything but the sunset, clutching her horse. Oh gods, to rain unprovoked violence on something, someone! Certainly the judge would get her a secret automobile, though she had wrecked the bicycle and left it in the pine barrens in her spite. Nitburg feared for her life, and was frankly afraid of automobiles himself.

Oh but for the wind in my hair, the cock of a gun or whatever you call it in my hand, the thrashing putrid smoke around me!

And in town she would buy another hat, too, the one with Spanish doubloons around the crown in Nell's Finery.

★

Able-bodied, thought dismal Fernando. What a dream. What a pest of a word now. His crippled knees had just barely unswollen and he hadn't the energy or the footage to walk over to that woman Stella with the knife scar on her face he so admired. Little Stella, just down the row, was centuries away and his desire, worming out from his cruel knees, was a hunched nullity. The pain in his knees reached right up through his gut, and near broke his heart. Acute of the acute, he mourned. Too, all this wrath for a mere nub of a villain. Fernando could not remember having insulted the tiny man. He'd never even stared at Smoot like the others. He recalled that once, drunk, he'd gone so far as to lobby for the oppressed Smoot in the saloon. Or thought he recalled that late afternoon, sunset on the French doors. Sad, sad, he was deeply sad. He had forgotten what sadness intense physical pain brought on. What could he accomplish? Alone, he screamed out, "You think I can stand this? Thrown in here with my pointless mental life? God damn it." Must he become something on the telephone, pestering the Reverend and Doc Fingo for his ointments and dope? Who wrote in stone this guano about his fate? What was the way out? By God, these wild days don't allow for any convalescence — history is running outside the window like a rapid, thieving raccoon. Coon Soon Die, sounded like the late plague in China, and almost every Chinese was named something like that. Get me some Indian medicine, have me an old Indian in here that knows something. He rose, trembling. Look at this, a man on two canes and I can't bear that. Fernando had a slight lisp. — *Sfuck,* he said. Then fell back on the chairs. This tarpaper hovel with one window after all my travels? With the Chinese standing around and wanting it back, those poor yellow bastards — dispossessed because they think I have some bullets left. The rain snarling down and Main Street a swine wallow. He looked to his weapon in the black holster. It had been a long time since he'd thought of bullets. The thing used a forty-five caliber, as he remembered. It had been a hell of a long time since he'd shot anybody. Much more of this agony and there might be one to the brain, doubt you not, swore Fernando.

The nittering Chinese were sometimes louder than the rain. He had thrown them out of this shack, and now raved at them to fetch drink and Doc Fingo. The eggs and soda crackers were laboring too long in his stomach, and there was no satisfaction. The growling longitude of his intestines, the spit in the throat like a piece of iron, his eyes feeling like worn holes. In his health he could scheme, plunge through, grapple, pitch and desist, sleeping like a housecat afterwards. But now . . . ow, ow! There is no hell like the enforced idleness of a born idler. Run to ground with his haunted memories — prison in the bad territorial prison. The ignominy of sledging away naked and chained in the Louisiana salt dome, the disgrace of a rattler bite near Van Horn, Texas, when he was resting on the ground and the snake just came up and bit him on the mouth, and since then, the despised lisp. The afternoon he'd stolen the mail from Wells Fargo and then wept over the letters to loved ones he had deflected, all those pages around him in a dry blowing wind under a trestle. Little brook under it about the amount of his tears. Collected exactly twenty-three dollars out of one hundred letters.

Then there was his Irish Catholic mother who believed in him and wept beyond her rheumatism and neuralgia, with her letters so heartfelt when he was in prison. And to whom he barely wrote once a year.

His father crushed by the railroad car in Lafayette, murdered by his own work.

He studied his red hound in the corner. Even the dog he could give nothing but noodles left behind by the Chinese and an occasional egg boiled on the

Franklin stove. For himself, he mashed in a clove of garlic. There was some money in the barn on his uncle's place, but it was far away and he couldn't use a runner, not in this treacherous town. The man would be found lying under a cactus with his throat slit. The water in the jug was getting stale. The whiskey was growing disconsolate.

At college he could do a bottle a day, merry and bright, up in the morning and out to loaf at the crack of seven, the booze sweet and iniquitous in his gullet. Never let him down even through the rare lectures he attended. Fernando smiled weakly. In those days his home was a covered wagon in a grove banked by cedars, all next to two springs bursting with icy spume from a mass of marble. He recollected the shaded swimming hole, near fatal with chill, in which he swam naked with the first female graduate in biology in all vast Dixie, or said she was. No mighty looker, but a fortune in laughter and reason behind those spectacles. Her children were the plants and animals and she required no penetration. What a fool mistake to cock your hat and loins toward mere pulchritude, Fernando suddenly thought. Every beauty he'd ever known had an infinite selfishness to her, and my god the pissing and moaning as if constantly displaced from the Ritz.

Then he let go a howl for his knees. These things were too damned real. When he got to the dwarf, through tornado, typhoon, swine-wallow mud, red tape, whatever, when he . . .

A negro in rags and brogans came into the door out of the rain. He held a bottle and a syringe and a covered dish on a tray.

— Who are you? asked Fernando.

— Miss Stella sent the dish and Doc Fingo the rest. He say you be knowin' how to minister the painkiller. Say it work quicker in a arm vein.

— I don't even rate a visit from the old fraud himself? I had a few kneecap questions. Can't you get him down here?

— He be in research say tell you.

— He be in search of his own asshole.

— Où sont les neiges . . . ?

— What'd you say?

— I from New Orleans too. You know what I said, Mister Muré.

— I thought you were playing with me.

— Miss Stella coming down with her dominoes some time tonight.

— Lord bless her. You ever been bored, Nicholas?

— Only when I breathe, Fernando. Ennui be my middle name but I moves it from place to place.

— You see my dilemma, then.

The door opened wide to the yakking, nittering Chinese and the angry rain. It hit the roof and Fernando saw the negro Nicholas go out like a hunk of night lost at sea.

Downwind from the saloon Fernando could hear the piano and the shouts of a dozen rancid trailmen moving back and forth — getting, spending, losing and hooting, occasionally a woman's voice, perhaps Stella's.

Shrill and indignant — impetuous hand or mouth on an unwarmed slut. The crowd — he could hear — was joined by filthy longriders who, by their accents, were Swedes from Minnesota down for the last of the Pony Hunt. He was missing all this. Why, he could be low too. He favored walking into a covey of harmless alley-corner negroes and commanding them, "Break it up! Break it up! All right now!"

— What we done, boss Nando?

— Just *being* negroes, Rastus. We have laws here, heh heh.

Pity, his southern side sometimes, taking over like that, but men became mean when it was ninety-five in the shade. Boredom arose on stilts, sweaty with vitriol. Less and less lung, less and less heart. Big drop of sweat popping out on a Gila monster, that's how hot.

After the injection, Fernando dreamed of reptiles and armadillos born out of his thigh, more agony and throes. There was a woman on a stage, shivering with sweat, removing one garment after another, twitching like a zombie — heartlessly. — Isn't this enough? Aren't you tired, tired? she said in the nude. Then she began removing her skin and hair. All of this clouded with rain and Chinese nittering.

★

The hermit Nermer could see it all from the lip of his mountain hole. It had stopped raining, and the town of Nitburg spread out under him like the toys of a giant. The great black cloud was breaking up at his feet. The vanity of those little roofs poked out. He could not hate, though, the long rectangle of the saloon. They could have named the saloon Nermer for the amount of whiskey and dice money he had spent there, before he was a hermit with his mule and Bible, ascending the rocky path upward, as if somebody cared when he threw away worldly things. The zigzagged path of the incline was rugged, but there *was* a path, he'd noticed. It was dangerous, but somebody had been along before.

He had worn his burlap suit and cheap boots with no socks, mortifying the flesh, but did anyone even give him a passing glance except Nandina, the judge's daughter, whom he had lain with drunkenly thrice? She was at the clothier's, stomping out on the plank gangwalk in new high black boots, and a new black lambskin shirt, and pants with a kind of Paris skirt — rich gray — around her waist. Some kind of cowgirl of high fashion so far ahead of these parts that it looked damned silly. He preferred to turn away from her silliness and ascend with her concerned look on his back. It was awfully good, however, that *somebody* had paid attention when he made his statement, because to be a hermit meant you spent ninety percent and more of your time seeking *food* and water and resisting masturbation and staring at rocks and odd crawling high-elevation life.

He ate the mule, his pal, within two weeks. Then went into contrition for a week, not to mention violent indigestion, having to run away and poot so as not to skunk up his homestead. To the left, thirty yards away, was a more comfortable hole in the mountain, but he had achieved a sort of permanence here in the worse hole; even a child, though, would have chosen the larger hole with its chairs of natural stone, a rift at the top — practically a ready-made fireplace with drawing capacity, the natural kitchen of stalagmites with a fresh brook running through — which would also make a nice sewer, and a big den where a bear used to be before a former hermit, Raving Mick, had run it out previous to his suicide. He kept it as a dream and did not need it.

Over and over he read the Twenty-third Psalm from the Holy Bible. This was the only verse a man needed, really. He read aloud every morning at sunrise, with the magpies and two mountain goats, married to each other, standing almost preposterously on the incline together, faithful and not lecherous, not low, mean, bitching, crying, pissing or moaning, merely handsome man and wife goats together, hearing the Twenty-third Psalm and then when Nermer finished, leaving on their beautiful feet as the black and white magpies rose on their wings with the message. — David, David, my psalmist, Hermit Nermer said with tears falling down. — Keep me on this mountain with my true friends. Even unto the little mice and spiders.

The town was wide open — with the black cloud having rushed back to its fellows. It was vain, miniature, but profound to him, and he could forgive them for their little risen structures. Also he had had the best sexual favor in town, Nandina, and what was there after that but meditation, the song of the mountain air, and needing less and less until he shrank into a man the size of an eye — pure vision — with wings on it, like his envied magpie friends.

He loved Fernando. There was something in the man. He looked down at the tarpaper shack standing desolate, its own Chinese slum, so tiny and alone and with a moat of spangling rainwater around it now — but to hermit Nermer's flying eye it harbored a great meaning. Nermer had cognition. From Fernando there was something moving, something coming. Nermer was suddenly pigeon-toed from excitement. Fernando had promised to burn the town once when he was drunk, and Nermer wished it would be so, be so, be so. He hopped in the remainder of his cheap boots. Be so. Be so!

★

The twin sheriffs Neb and Dantly suddenly met each other. Neb Lewton still had memories and left a trail of rust from his pants in the chair seat and across the floor, where he had hobbled to feed

Quick, his Welsh spaniel. Some days Neb, who'd killed a man with a gun thirty years ago, thought about himself as a youth. But killing the one man had thrown him over like a surf wave on the coast of San Diego where the greasers jumped off the pier and were swept into a salty foam. His twin Dantly was a weak swaybacked man with a lot of attitudes, but the town was so busy in graft, gambling and whoring that they thought it was Neb doing his rounds. Dantly would shoot, just out of nervous habit. He would shoot a harmless dog on the corner just sleeping there, old Fido in the dust, tired of running. He drilled him, and then some ladies of the church came out and congratulated him for cleaning the streets. The person Neb Lewton, however, appeared to receive the reward.

Judge Nitburg, there with his riches and paranoia, came up trembling, growing balder and uglier by the minute. Truth serum had been invented recently and the judge was so nervous he even forgot to get fellatio from his old wife Agnes. In the old days he could just ram it in and be forgotten, all his lies and secrecy behind him like the diarrhea of a millionaire. Some afternoons the judge was so exquisitely friendless that he rolled over and over in a hot tub of water trying to suck himself. Threw water out of the tub. He had another vicious migraine and had summoned the sheriffs. Dantly and Neb came in the house, rust falling out of Neb's gun and the old bullets close to his butt. The judge wanted to be shot. He couldn't stand the pain anymore. The judge was in his robe, all wet and wrung out, as if having swum from Galveston.

The sheriffs refused to shoot him, though neither of them cared for the man. Neb might be a useless, ancient man with gruesome corpulence, but he would not shoot a man with a migraine, whatever that was. It must be some pain in the head. There was a problem of shooting him in the head since so many jobs and so much graft depended on him, for one thing. Nitburg seemed able to buy away everything. At Christmas and Easter he would deliver a bunch of foodstuffs to orphans and Chinese, hence possessing them, in a way, further.

Well, it was always Neb Lewton's talent to turn away and go home for a good meal, hanging the gun up with a gasp on a hook. He was near suicide himself and often thought of getting a chair and hooking himself to the brain and falling off dead with his eye strung out and what gut there was from the eye to the brain prolonging some vision until he got to heaven and had that *really good* meal — with his one friend, the old boy he'd shot thirty years ago. He had in mind a trough of lobsters and fried yams.

★

The Reverend was giving his last speech to himself, here in the church and nearly alone. He was about to die from horniness and love of Christ, together.

For Nandina, who would not give him a serious look. For Christ, who was his own age when He died and forgave them all. The Reverend did not have enough energy or vigilance to pursue the wrong things anymore; lately, too, he'd gotten a raw deal on his skin and increasing bodily hair. My God, what am I supposed to be, a *skunk* with black hair piling off me, a godforsaken *wereman*? Give me release, Old Master, from this vale of tears. My vale of late and growing hair where there is no relief. I've been exceptional in my business as a big fish in a small pond here, Great Fisherman. Yes, cut back my arrogance, but I've gone around for five years with an erection the like of which must be hidden by some exorbitantly long coat — and my head won't even stay steady anymore without a hat. Holiness, however, does fill my head when the trumpet and the piano and the cymbals and the voice of Bernice lift the hymns — Fernando standing right outside the stained-glass window, adding his very extra-sweet voice, lonely and brave, even in what must be his terrible hangover and guilt. My God uses so many of us as instruments to bring His love home, home. Where is home when I get paler, uglier, hairier and more breathless every day? Where is the place, Lord?

Please, I don't want to meet every hideous fool I've ever met, don't say we'll all have to be there in heaven like that. I could not bear mine own self at a heavenly convention. You must not give us that supreme music too often, Lord. I am begging to not be accepted into heaven now. I am begging you to stop this eruption of hair and rash. Is Satan the master here? Is the laughing Fiend the master of our streets? I shall not allow this. Perhaps the death of Judge Nitburg, our rear-pew benefactor. What can I offer, what more rules can I announce, before your Grace falls into church like a sequoia?

Reverend McCorkindale had earlier officiated at a service; but Fernando was not at his usual place, outside the stained-glass window singing off his hangover. What was wrong?

The sun had come up sharply after the rains of the last three days. Old Mrs. Nitburg was continuing the hymn behind him. Nobody had come through the mud for her yet. They were given a hard crust to walk on with a three-foot-deep world of mud with hogs in it beneath them.

When he strode out of the church, there was a family ahead in a buckboard, only their heads visible, inching along. Their young were disguised as children. There was no expression at all on these Mormon young.

This is a foul town in all regards, thought the Reverend. And I daily fouler in it. He was wading in the crust as a hog erupted. His sexual guilt was about to overcome him when he saw dry land in front of the saloon. There was another dry path toward the tarpaper shack with the Chinese off in mud knee deep, protesting around the doorway where Fernando was sewing a poncho out of canvas with a large needle while smoking a Mexican cigarette.

Reverend McCorkindale stumbled as a great wind came up. His face was red and welted, angry over his new hair. He called in, "Could I have a look at you, my friend?"

Fernando brightened toward the voice.

— If you can stand this broken-down society, Reverend.

— I can, I can. I believe we are twins in misery.

The Reverend sat on the cot, a board with a quilt fixed on two sawhorses. Little Stella moaned and rolled to the side with a sigh. McCorkindale had not noticed her sleeping. She was still in her shoes, her lavender pumps shot with silvery thread. The girl stayed dead in her dreams. The preacher, filthy with mud from the thighs down, shoved to one side and caught up the whiskey bottle held out by Fernando. He gave himself a rough and sudden splash. Instantly he felt the vastness of his own dreams, a sort of smiling lust for heaving nude angels.

— You seen Smoot? asked Fernando.

— He wasn't at the service.

— He will need consolation, soon.

— They say he's out of the county, searching for something, most likely an automobile. The man seeks internal combustion.

— Which would set him around my Uncle Navy's spread. I don't like that. Here with my cursed knees. Say . . . He peered closer in to the cheeks of McCorkindale. — Are you raising a beard?

It seemed the Reverend's forehead wanted to participate, too, a scatter of black hairlings racing

34

for the scalp from the eyebrows. The man was reading for the law nights and seemed to be letting himself go. McCorkindale blanched and poured more whiskey into his red mouth.

— God hates me, Muré. An animal thing is happening to me. Tears rolled out of his eyes.

— Hold on. Thought you and the Lord were thick.

— There must be something deep down queer and wrong.

Fernando looked back to his roughly stitched poncho. Outside the sky was darkening again. The four-hour blazing sun in the morning seemed a perverse demonstration. Like the poncho he was working on while his legs were useless. What did he know of stitching? The muck outdoors frightened him. His unbathed body seemed dangerous as well, all of a sudden. Be damned, the drug was running out and he could feel it leaving like a Kansas City train with a last hoot round the bend into the alien hills. He had the Fear. You didn't want a preacher to talk like that. He needed more of the drug and he did not hesitate to awaken little Stella. He gave her almost all the rest of his money. He asked her if she could bring a fried chicken back for the Reverend and him, though he had no appetite at all. He made her a cup of black coffee off the stove and kissed her without passion full on the mouth.

She was tubercular and brittle. She could be snapped right in two. He dearly loved the gasping naughtiness left to Stella now that the final hours seemed upon her. They made a pair, didn't they? Barely a spare part of motility left to either of them. This old friendship left from the hot vigors of yesteryear with the hound sleeping in the bed afterwards. Give us your little cough and apologetic smile, my toy pet. But please be prompt with Fingo and the drug. He put the poncho on her. For gloves she was wearing a fresh pair of Fernando's wool socks. The preacher paid for another bottle. Fernando was curious about himself. He could not bear whiskey any longer.

The Reverend said when she'd left:

— How about producing the guitar and let's try to sing one?

Fernando looked at his own chest. — I don't think there's anything there, McCorkindale.

— "I Walk in the Garden Alone"?

— That's for them that can walk. I can hardly tumble toward the outhouse.

Outside, the Chinese moaned and remonstrated.

★

It was raining where Smoot sat his enormous ashy horse. Persimmons were on the ground all around him, and the tree partly hid him from the house, a U of speckled, varnished blond logs. He moved his telescope from the house to the barn door, through which he could see the automobile. Inside the house Fernando's uncle was playing with something that moved. That ain't right, there ain't nothing supposed to be like that, white and black and upright, he

36

thought behind the round vision in the glass. Navy was prancing in the window with the creature, first caressing, then kissing it. The creature ran out of sight before Smoot realized it was a monkey. He was stunned, heartstruck. His little feet curled in their boots, almost something like lust in him. Some elves' magic told him the being was female.

What a promise to have that thing beside me in Navy Remington's automobile! The driving apparatus could be cut down, dwarfized, and you could melt steel onto it, with a prow for roaming, great and dangerous! Natural law should yank that automobile right out from under him and put that monkey square on the seat beside me. The three of us — auto, monkey, and me — would be *beyond, then.*

Nobody could say anything, just like you can't say much about a cyclone — it's just there and it ain't up to your opinion. Or it *was* there, and even if you move a word or two out of your puny mouth like "What a hell of a thing!" it ain't never no real part of nothing, because the cyclone is what was.

Them others wouldn't even know Smoot was in view — like now, astride his giant ashy steed. He was growing tall underground, toward the center of the earth amongst everything marvelous that was never seen. His brow was cooled by underground springs and his legs were white as a mushroom and it didn't hurt at all. The hell with the sun and the tallards with their shifty crotches, about all he normally saw of them. He had that perpetual crack in the neck from looking upwards. But nah, it didn't hurt at all underground.

He had spied on Remington a great deal before — five times, indeed — and was used to his movements. So he was patient, especially with the new monkey. Navy Remington was a man of the ocean.

★

Sometimes he would book ship in Galveston, steaming to Brazil. Whence the monkey. He was an old man now, sixty-two, like Judge Nitburg, a contemporary in too many ways. The judge wanted to take care of that. Remington had the pictures and knew the things. At any second he could drive into Nitburg and the judge's court itself and blow the town wide open, the judge and his blind patroness out on a buckboard at night toward Mexico before the smoldering town overflowed itself out to his manse and reviled him. There were still plenty of old Rebels here and others with honor, though they were cowardly nowadays.

Smoot clicked his tongue on the roof of his mouth, as he did most of the day, so a little nickering sound popped out of his realm while he dreamed of the picture, the things, the revulsion of the town, the rambling buckboard, the smoke of South Texas dust, himself ramming through it in the long steely automobile, beyond it all, circling it, the monkey in goggles sitting next to him. He would mount two steel barrels of gasoline in the back seat so he would never run out of fuel. He could drive to Brazil and meet that monkey's relatives if he wanted to.

There wasn't going to be no passengers in *this* automobile — only two earnest pilots. Eat our dust, caballeros.

Remington left the house much later this time. It was three in the afternoon. All that daylight automobile time wasted. Smoot could not understand it. But sure enough he came out with the monkey sitting trained on his shoulder without a rope or chain on it. It looked permanent and wise on his shoulder, more like the monkey was conducting the old man than the contrary. Remington was stepping around some peafowl droppings and barking at the big lustrous birds, who hustled away as in Brazil, Smoot guessed. The monkey must be telling Remington to scold them useless hussies. There ain't much else in the world now I'm here, you could bet she was saying. Smoot's eyes watered thinking of her gentle monkey directions. The sun caught the brilliant white fur of her stomach and at her hands and feet, with the pink big-eyed face solemn, the rest coal black like a deep blanket. Smoot near perished with tender feelings for the little beast. What a cunning little pal she'd be! The wind whipping by, her little eyes in goggles, a dustcoat matching his, the smoky wake of the machine behind them!

Then Smoot became sullen in his duty. The automobile leapt out of the barn with smoke like a disaster pouring on the ground. Remington and the monkey were left to vision. Smoot put the telescope viciously back in its case, almost knocking himself over with ire. The car raced off to the west. Toward Nitburg, Smoot guessed. Remington could afford the hideously inflated prices of the grocery over there. Smoot poisoned his garden every solstice. Navy Remington might have been a big man on the sea, but he was a fool moving his garden from place to place in a sublime watered meadow. Probably looking up at the sky toward God and asking what the deuce were these last two years, Papa? Smoot smiled, but not very much.

He would have to ride down to the house and look for the pictures again. The only bright spot was if he found them, the judge was practically *his*. But he had gone over the premises before. They were neat in a military way, with all the moveables nailed down as in quarters full ahead on the high seas. Neither plush nor mean, the house had a quality of collected bachelor habit. There was a Bible, an insect collection, a telescope on a tripod at the bay window overlooking a plat with a little river curling through banks of purple sage and buttercups. The old man liked his flora. Tulips bloomed around the whole house. Next to the kitchen door were two great banana plants. Smoot judged that there was too much damned sissy prettiness around the place, like some spic's flower wagon had blown up. Or like some imported woman was around here. He touched his little pistol in case somebody else was in the house.

Whoa, here was something new. In the study, in

a locked glass case, was a thick moroccan-bound logbook with a piece of white tape running across it, printing on it: *The History of My Life and Times by Capt. A. Navy Remington.*

Smoot was no locksmith, nor could he leave a loose clue about his searchings in these rooms, else the old man would barricade the premises and impact somebody with that old Winchester over there. The afternoon would be over. But what kind of pompous scrivener would leave this thing locked under glass, title up? He must have an enormous strutting idea of his life and times. That log was just gloating there without a speck of dust on it, insulting the trespasser. The judge would worry. There were droves of eastern press men covering the Wild West for such as this, Smoot knew.

He sifted through what was loose or stacked for a while, but there was nothing of the pictures. Also not a speck of money, hard or soft. The old man had buried it or carried it with him, what he didn't have in that New Orleans bank.

Then Smoot came to the room he suspected he would come to, and he was burned down by jealousy. The monkey had a room to itself. Remington had crafted it a small bed, an elegant crib with a pillow and fringed Mexican bedspread on it. There were rubber rats and frogs on the floor. Bananas and nuts were in a canister. The room smelled a little sour but there were no droppings around. Suddenly he was infuriated, and raced out of the home to the outhouse, expecting that wonderful and queer thing, and there it was when he yanked open the door: a new blond plank, a double-holer. One large for a human and the other miniature for a monkey, with a box of tissues between them. This was so *cute*! He could hardly stand it. The monkey should be his and that was all there was to it.

That old rich man has . . . everything and more, and me, me! Turd of the gods. Smoot began weeping. All philosophy had run out of him. He took off his great hat. His curls tumbled down to his wet eyes, and he wept with big shudders.

At the last he saw to his nose with his bandana.

If he *lives* to have it, brooded Smoot. Or something don't happen to him.

★

Nandina could not figure it out, quite. The wretched Smoot, even more the insect from this distance to her bare eye, stood for half an hour outside the outhouse door, hat in hands, barely moving except for here and there a kick at the soil. He seemed to be going through some temper and priss. She'd ridden up to the persimmon tree exactly in time — blast it! — to see the auto depart to the west in front of a cone of dust, sunset bound. She had called in sick to the schoolhouse, freeing herself of the children for a day. True, it was her time of the month, but more, she direly needed a ride in Remington's auto. She had speculated even romancing the man, if the old bachelor required it.

She was wearing her new black hat with the

Spanish doubloons circling the crown. She knew she was fetching, though this hat and band of coins was heavy and she took it off her sweating forehead while the palomino munched the persimmons behind her. The auto removing to the horizon gave her a pang square in the lair of love and she was hit by a powerful cramp. She was not used to a horse this long in the hills and her back hurt too. But here was Smoot, fretting himself.

She smiled, because under her her wonderful legs were in no trouble at all, straining to run quick into iniquity or wherever adventure demanded. My word, I must be good, she grinned, I ran Nermer clear up in the mountain to a hermithood. He was a handsome brawny lover, too. But here was Smoot, frozen to weird space, ignoring the great roan who moped around the tulips of the blond place.

She wanted him out of there and she must not be seen, now that Remington and the automobile were gone.

Nermer, once a bosom buddy of Fernando's, had one night come on to her so charged with whiskey and spunk that he had grown quite a tongue on him. He had whispered the secret of Fernando's "something" in the "barn" just before urging his sperm into her the third time, then hanging aside like a morose rag doll. He wished to hell he hadn't spoken, and she could see the hate for her striking from his eyes. But there would always be a bit of barter when a man had his delight with you, even when you enjoyed the thrusting yourself. The secret was misty anyway. Something hidden and important to a man might just be a box of old love letters — as from that bespectacled, scientific drab Fernando was so fond of knowing back at "college."

Nandina once heard a song about this woman from below the saloon window — wondering whose sweet voice it was, until she heard the inept guitar and knew it was the drunken Fernando himself, her wanted one, perhaps her intended.

At last Smoot left, almost never climbing the saddle of the big roan, a bent puppet completely ignored by the horse, who took the auto road and finally got out of eyesight.

Why am I so bound and determined to get things? Nandina asked before the thought could be prevented. The palomino was lowering gracefully toward the barn and she moved, a glorious woman with tangled hair, down with it. In *McGuffey's Reader* it said the wind was tempered to the shorn lamb. But the same advice from the deity, should it go to the pirate and his cutlass on the hopeless virgin with her multiple petticoats and little slippers, her father the Captain, both of them soon dead despite his elegance? Oh, how Nandina imagined. Maybe these thoughts came from her unknown and gone mother, because she couldn't remember ever not thinking them. But there was not even a picture of her mother to be seen. What was her mama like? She must have been a whirlwind. Accidentally, during one of his migraine attacks, Nandina had seen the immense naked member of Judge Nitburg, and that condemned her, she reckoned, maybe even biblically. She could not stop the wonder about who in hell she *was* — the fury of that thing in her mother, already dreaming of life among the vicious Comanches, as her father had confessed. The next day he'd walked calmly to the Dolores Springs signs east and west, torn them down, and nailed up two new signs with the name *Nitburg* on them.

His old blind wife had cackled with glee and her giant son had come over to protect the signs before the rigged vote for the new changed name was in. That brute so tall, muscular and ugly he was a gender unto himself. You wouldn't provide intercourse for that thing with heaven in the bargain.

Nandina was in the barn now, afoot and stroking the noses of Remington's stock. So, she thought, apparently I can't bear children. Otherwise, I would be swarmed under by Nermer's brood. And so I must bring forth things and adventures. Things and adventures are the fruit of my womb and there is nothing I can do about it. — Is there, girl? She spoke to the mare in the barn. — Thank God horses can't talk. But I wish, pretty thing, you could tell me where the goodies are.

She looked in the stalls and kicked around in the familiar aroma of manure and sweet hay and dusty oats. Not to dirty her swell black boots and sterling tips, though.

You really needed a man out here with a pickax. For surely it was underground. She went up the ladder and kicked at the bales but there was nothing there, as imagined. She let herself down and began staring, hoping her gaze would collect some fortune to it. God, give the best of your Comanche stargazers, their priest roaming out from some butte, give me some talkative astronomy all above them and my mother, too, calling out to me from the Indians. Give me your best.

She saw the slick of oil where the car had been. It pooled in hard clay, a bowl, where about an inch of the stuff glistened like a dark rainbow. Walking to it and kneeling, she noticed a boxy depression of soil and kicked away the straw and pea gravel until she was sure, then stood across the boxy depression with the pool of motor oil right in the middle of it. There was something down there all right. She could not know the beauty of her widened raiding eyes. Dark-balled and hot like an Indian's.

She knelt and put her fingers in the oil, right down to the clay. Then she put a finger in her mouth. This was a first for her. So this was what made the New World run. There was something awfully familiar about the taste, something from way back there in the swamps, the gas, the rotten roots, the scaly alive things heaving mud around. She put her finger in again and sucked the oil off.

Actually, she thought, this tastes better than men.

★

In the night when she passed the shack, which the Chinese called "House of the Afflicted" — still crouched around it, wanting back in — she heard the ailing voices of Muré and McCorkindale, puny with drug and drink, struggle toward harmony around a wretched commotion on the guitar. The songs spoke of loss in vast spaces and moony crouching near rocks and sinkholes; woe, terror and defeat. "How yellow the heart!" she heard distinctly. The men were blind with chemicals.

Someone told her that Fernando had had his knees broken some weeks back. You could hear it in his voice — a coward's pouting at the universe. The sickness in McCorkindale's voice was remarkable, too, though this man could never sing squat anyway. What disgrace she heard from Muré. It was said that the man had dancing testicles named Manuel and Juan, but there was no believing it in this sorry crooning. "The yellow lizard lurketh nigh! Color of my sigh!" McCorkindale sang backup — "My God! My God!" over and over.

She stepped back into alley shadows as Doc Fingo hurried past her from the door of the shack, a kit in his hand. The Chinese parted. A morose wind came down the street with tumbleweeds and the smell of whiskey from the saloon. Nandina was nevertheless happy, though nervous in her thighs. The alley, the Chinese, even the bad music — they were hers, they bore her name. The soil of it was all over her and her hands smelled like oil. She clasped the handle of the great dagger she wore with her riding gear. How sublime it felt.

"Yellow mucus was her name!" moaned from the window. Inside, she could see that little tubercular slut sitting on a cot, blowing bass notes in the neck of a quart bottle. You'd best keep the air you've got, thought Nandina. Shadows of the trio flickered from the coal oil, flame of catastrophe.

★

1911

— There used to be gunplay here. There's hardly any now, you notice.

— Yes, your worship.

— Actually there wasn't much . . . play. People shot each other, from the back at close range, preferably. One true pistolero came in the territory, you wouldn't hear a peep for weeks. You could say I was the first to introduce . . . an unpistoled dwarf as . . . regulator. You can't just have Law, Smoot. You've got to have something *of the night,* you understand?

— Yes sir.

— Well, take pride. But still nothing from Remington's place?

— Nothing. Smoot lied in a way. There was the monkey, dear captive of Remington.

— Remington came in this afternoon with a damned monkey riding in the seat next to him in that car you covet.

Smoot's eyes watered.

— Lonely bachelor fool. Pitiful simian for company. He'll be full over the loon farm come nigh. People won't believe a damned thing from him . . . Nothing at all. Not the slightest suggestion . . . A monkey.

48

— There ain't intrinsically nothing wrong with a monkey, your worship, really.

— What?

— A man . . . a person could have a monkey.

— Are you hurt? Why're you wet?

— Out at his house. Something hurt me.

— Does it hurt, by the way, Smoot, to be . . . short?

Smoot was enraged. — That old man's writing the story of his life and times. He ain't cuckoo.

Judge Nitburg narrowed his eyes and blanched. The blood of migraine roared from some gland and bumped his noggin. His right eye drooped and his right nostril filled with slime. It was as if a wire heated from his eye to his gut, came back, and blew off the right side of his head. Stars burst in his vision. Nausea gripped him. His upper lip shone and curled.

Smoot knew what was happening. He dried up immediately, cuff to eyes.

— His house is neat as a pin. The barn, you could eat in it. He's an ace carpenter and an autopilot, drives that automobile. He planted out them tulips. Must be patient as a monk.

— Christ, stop it!

— Course if you'd rather hear he's out there tuppin' his sheep with his seacap on backward, I . . .

— Cursed man sailed all around the world, all over the world, and wound up in *my own* backyard.

— Something could happen if I had the automobile . . . and the monkey. Something could happen.

— Ow! Ow!

— The vehicle would have to be cut down.

— See to it! Don't just hang around being . . . Ow! Whoa!

The judge thrust away to the dark rear shadows of the manse.

— Get Fingo! the tiny voice called out to Smoot, like a cat in a well.

Back on his transportation, Smoot barely kicked the horse. It moved out like an inchworm. Smoot's mind was hot with cunning and any speed would destroy this rapture.

★

The magpies flocked around Nermer the hermit, too many of them. Mountain goats nibbled among the crevasses while magpies rode their backs. Mountain mice shot back and forth, rustling. Magpies were on his feet and shoulders. Great mountain armadillos shouldered out of the cave, as if it were theirs. Others, hitherto unknown relatives, rocked by him without a nod. Word of his gentleness had traveled to all the wee and big folk of the timberline.

Nermer strolled the precipice.

He should be looking everywhere else, but he gazed down at Nitburg. The town was ugly and sad, but he could not keep his eyes off it. He had not achieved real hermithood and he knew it, yet there was no book written for this occupation. He had abandoned women, whiskey, smoke, his soft bed, his soft wool socks. All for vision, rapture, solitude. But look where he was looking. Right at the miserable anthill itself. It was not so much the sin but the paltry times there that disgusted him. He had been high, wide and handsome down there, but to what avail? With the goons of make-do staring at him over their dominoes? Skinny coyotes of the spirit.

Even Nandina, very deliberate in her "surrender." Her father might be a monster, as they said, but was there even the possibility of a monster in a town of mountain mice? Nandina and her cupidity. He'd been with her over and over. Something was knocked down in him. An exhausted depression followed that never snapped up for him. A refractory gloom, a morbid disaster in the belly. Nermer wondered whether there was always, in the heart of an arsonist, a woman on fire in the middle of the buildings. A gorgeous devastator with now her comeuppance from the aggrieved. Or if men — Christians especially — loved that vision of the flaming earth at the End because their bad loves and bad mothers were burned up.

He would not have to look at that town anymore when Fernando burned it down. It would burn the woman, his own sins, his own paltriness. He could then return his gaze to the mountains and the heavens and be about his hermithood. He could go about "his father's business," as the Carpenter said. He of the whip and the sword as well as the humble donkey and the meek lamb.

Nermer considered his own mother, a vicious, callous pioneer who could neither read nor write nor barely talk. Nor eat, with only her gums left toward the end. The concept of either humility or pride would never have occurred to her mind. Mind? Mind? All she had was mean habits — a protesting hunk of dust in motion. There was a "party" once in the squalid huts near the red stream where they lived. Someone was "having a party." One person had a jug, brought from far away in Kentucky. Another had a Jew's harp. They cleaned their clothes in the stream, combed their hair, and some ancient thing with an Irish memory rose and squatted as the harp plucked away, a "dance," although the old man wasn't raising dust. His mother stood out front from the hut for a while, spat on the ground, and went back in to tear apart a chicken. She did not know what a party was, nor what Kentucky was, nor what the man was doing with the fart-sounding iron thing in his mouth. As for the cooking, it was fast, vicious and terrible. For fifteen years they did not have a vegetable. She had scurvy, tuberculosis, piles, and never noticed anything until the stroke lamed and blinded her. Some man of the cloth, or formerly of the cloth, presided at the funeral, but after opening the Book several times, he couldn't find anything to read or say. So they just named the settlement for her: Dead. Later on a poet came through the place and they changed the name to We The Living, New Mexico.

For years after his mother died, Nermer would

have a colorful dream in his sleep and awake with horrid guilt, as if he'd somehow violated the rules. Later on, he shot an Apache child in a wide desert for getting in his way. Along with his gun, he sported a maroon leather outfit that burned him up in the sun. What was he to do, leave the outfit on that Mexican found dead of thirst in the other desert two weeks ago? Leave the long silver pistol and all those bullets in the fancy bandolier? He was very tired of hitting nothing with it on the byways, too. So he just shot the child.

Another thing about that outfit and pistol was that they had bought him an instant career in Nitburg with Fernando, who saw Nermer at the horse trough — buried in it, really — new in Nitburg and nearly dead of thirst. He drank and drank, staggered back to the ruts and the sun, and vomited water, which felt almost as good coming up as it did going down. A wet munificence spread through his stomach to his blood, and by the time Fernando saw him, walking his horse toward that tall, narrow, curious church at the end of the street, he might *have* revived to the hero that Fernando mistook him for.

— By damn, I always wanted to look like that. That's some suit and pistol.

Fernando was taller than he, with a merry white-toothed mouth under a long mustache, Mexican style, but he was obviously a tanned white man. Those hidalgos down there wore mustaches to differentiate themselves from mere Indians, who couldn't have mustaches. Nermer, unable to reply at first, just smiled.

— Ain't barely a point to the West if you can't have a beet-colored pistolero outfit like that, is there? With that silver hand-rifle.

Nermer noticed then that Fernando was drunk. He looked for a short-gun somewhere on him, expecting it now, in fact, because of his remorse about the Apache child. No gun on the man. He had a colorless serge coat on him and held a guitar in his gun hand like it was a negligent, small child. Still, the man had an alacrity about him when you thought he might suddenly produce a short-gun from the top of those old Sears Roebuck boots with the other hand. Bang. You are dead.

— What kind of church is that? asked Nermer.

— Kind of straight and narrow, isn't it?

— And tall. Four stories. Wood. With a bell.

— That's Reverend McCorkindale. Like he's daring a high wind, lightning, or fire, said Fernando. You can't ever tell. Something might happen. Jesus Himself turn up in a leather beet-colored pistolero suit.

The guitar flew from his right hand and Fernando did a backflip on the soil flat off the ground in front of Nermer. Next thing Nermer knew, his hat had flown backward and the barrel of a short-gun was in his mouth, Fernando smiling over him and himself thrown rearward with the man's other arm under his back, his own pistol cast away with his hand making a claw in the empty air for it.

— Jesus, even I couldn't miss you like this, could I? grinned Fernando.

— Please. Were you kin . . . to the child?

— What? Fernando threw the gun somewhere back in his coat and brought Nermer up straight.

— Hello, man, just polishing my practice. You get into weird steps with your idle time, like me. It doesn't mean a damned thing. Out West, you got all the time in the world to practice.

— I'm very glad, said Nermer, going to fetch his gun.

— We've got a pool table now. Old Judge Nitburg's bought a table and some cuesticks for the hotel. Muse is running it. Have a rack with me?

— What?

— A game. It's with sticks and balls, pockets in a table.

— Why not? If I could get a meal first?

Fernando bought him the beefsteak, potatoes and beans, with some kind of tasteless mushroom botany on the side.

They were chums thereafter. There was always the glossy and impossible glow around Fernando. Though he never pulled that insane feat with the pistol again, there was a constant dread that he might. Nermer was always a bit wary until the outfit rotted off him and the pistol was at Nitburg's pawnshop, gathering specks of rust. Then he was simply mild, high, wide and handsome, winning pool games from Mormons and that huge crowd of dusty idiots from Minnesota, who knew next to nothing about the marvelous game of eight-ball pool, elegant on a sweet rectangle of green felt, whisked clean by Muse and a smiling whiskered Chinee, Uncle Hsu.

The money is real, learned Nermer.

There is certainly something out there in Remington's barn. A lot else, Fernando told him. The guns and the money and pornography. Old Captain Remington, the wealthy, winking eccentric with the Winton Flyer. The old man had promised Fernando a motorcycle when he sobered up, too. Told him, though, he wasn't old enough to see the pictures yet.

Now Nermer could see almost to another county, to the east where Remington lived.

He'd come in Nandina and betrayed Fernando to her.

He was a sorry soul.

Here on the mountain with his cuestick as a crutch and helper, peering grimly at the odd church — a mere finger on a rise from his vantage with a cloud of magpies between. More his synagogue, the billiards room of the hotel twinkled·now as night came near, and he could imagine the balls clicking with wrath. Certainly some Minnesotan newly out of the tub, his hair slicked back with water and lilac, was picking his teeth, wide smile of a sucker on him. To be taken by the best in Texas, Randy Black. Now that he wasn't the shark in town, Black was.

★

Weeks later the man — who *was* that man? — was on his crutches beneath the lone stained-glass window of the church. He had dropped his mother's locket in the mud and was lowering himself to scrabble for it. His skin was yellow where it wasn't gray. On his back was a ragged orange shirt. His hair was long and black, with white streaks in it. As for his speech, he muttered as if he'd fallen into a stream of involuntary profanity. Church members heard him outside the window, a steady low raving and to the right of McCorkindale's sermon, which was incoherent itself. Something about larceny and revulsion. The preacher was in black, a black robber's kerchief on him, preaching under it, sucking in and blowing out. You could see nothing much but his eyes, hot and suffering.

— The Lord giveth and the Lord taketh away. Rotten Indian-giver, eh? McCorkindale was saying. — There is no mercy. Things can turn on you like a stomped snake.

Old Agnes Nitburg was smiling. Yes, yes. Preach on, beloved lad! The others, worn out by greed and bad diets, harked along sleepily.

Nandina sat by Agnes, drawing the long glances of her older male pupils, Highboy Warner and Clem Hook. These lads were devastated by Nandina. When they were out carp-fishing together, they never quit imagining her. They would save her from cannibals and then eat her themselves.

They would cut her loose from Geronimo, and then she would owe them something. Or they would catch her bathing in the Red Breaks — she was naked, and they would wear her clothes. She was very stern in the classroom, practically a kaiser. How they hated and wanted her, especially now in church with her bonnet on.

When McCorkindale would pause, you might hear the low mutter of Fernando outdoors. He had found his mother's locket and licked the mud off it. It was the last thing of value he possessed. Now he wore it, hung low from its thin gold necklace, and swung himself into a rut back to town. He made a sorry sight to the churchgoers exiting at noon, offering them this effeminate locket for sale. Pleading and cursing at the same time. Who *was* this man? What depths were necessary for him? Why didn't he drop his crutches and just wallow? This shabby orange rug of a man.

Old Agnes heard him. She, with her ankle-length hair, on the arm of a petulant Nandina. — Who is that man? she called. Nandina looked past Fernando at the splendid automobile of Navy Remington, parked on dry soil near the Nitburg Hotel.

There was fine coffee in the hotel, and Remington would travel a great distance for good coffee and a cheroot. Her astonished eyes retreated. Gosh, it was Fernando, all yellow and gray, a nasty stubble on his cheeks, the wind blowing him like a nasty kite. Crutches tormenting him.

— Take me to that man. I know him. In my mind I've known him somewhere.

— No, Agnes.

— Take me to him, horrid child.

She led the old woman near to Fernando, who was saying, "Ten? Ten dollars? Last of the estate." Then he went into his low muttering.

— I'll buy, my good man, said Agnes.

— N—

— Hand over this twenty, the old woman said, going at her purse. She could feel denominations with the tips of her fingers.

Fernando raised the locket, touching Agnes's hair. She purred. Another bill flashed toward him. It was doubtful Fernando recognized Nandina at all. Or rather, she saw, that he felt entirely hidden by his recent awfulness. A stale funk came off him, not alcoholic but awful nonetheless. He licked his lips and took to his crutches. Even his hat had been sold. His black-and-white hair streamed in the wind.

— Much obliged, much obliged.

— Who was he? asked Agnes.

— An old cripple. Something else is wrong with him, too.

— I've heard that voice . . . singing somewhere. You can't tell me.

★

Doc Fingo, out of church, saw Remington with his coffee and cheroot at a rear polished table of the hotel dining room. He had a punch at the bar, his hands shaking a bit. Fingo was a potbellied man with small weak legs. His feet were tiny too, in the natty laced ankle shoes of the day, but they had a thrill of fear in them. It ran up his thighs to his back. Remington was not conscious that the man was in the room. Other thirsty churchgoers had penetrated, calling for coffee or punch. He could not know he was haunting Fingo. Fingo was awfully glad for the crowd. His stethoscope was in his pocket. His watch chain was in place across his stomach. Was he not a respected man? Had he not kept watch over the smallpox plague a few years back? Had he not the pits of the scourge himself on his cheeks? Caught from that little orphan boy. In the mirror behind the bar was a proper man with the deep bagged eyes of experience — himself. The six weeks of medical study still told on him, he calculated. That was thirty-five years ago. There were proper aspects of him to cheer. He ordered another punch, and was near the last swallow when a hand grasped his shoulder. He saw in the mirror who the man was and quailed. It was Remington, smiling, with . . . some placid beast on his shoulder with its arms crossed like a schoolmarm. A monkey. Fingo's ivory-handled cane fell to the floor.

— Oops! Not to frighten, old sawbones, said Remington, stooping for the cane. The monkey mounted his head, perched on the white waves of hair. Even his hair seemed naval, in motion. The monkey then perched on Fingo's cane, out-stretched in Remington's hand.

— That's quite a piece of business, said Fingo.

— My little imp. Look at her.

— Is it dyed?

— Nah. Came out of its habitat like that.

— Don't it pee and poot on the floor?

— Seems like you the one leaking, Fingo.

It was true. His right shoe was wet, and the tip of his returned cane sat in his urine. Fingo was mortified.

— A resultant of the old pox, he said.

— No distress. You have a moment?

— Here?

— No. On the veranda, if you would.

Fingo bought another quick punch and followed the old captain to the veranda, where the wind was still stout. Up on the hill the church bell was clunking and rocking, an elevated and demoralizing *dong*. In the shadow of the tall church was the tarpaper shack, Fernando leaning at the door on his crutches, peering distinctly at Fingo and now more animated, raising one crutch and shaking it over the huddled Chinese.

— They say he's not drinking, said Remington.

— He won't visit me, so I have to listen to the talk about him.

— Broke knees. Bring a strapping man down.

— They say he can't stand water on his skin. The boy used to have a hot tub once a day. He loved it better than anything.

— A fellow that's down on himself'll change. I've studied many a depressed case . . .

— Why is he holding money up in the air, beckoning you?

— Maybe square his bill a bit. Been sort of carrying him. I ain't impatient. Man down on his luck, well . . .

— If you don't cure him, I'll kill you, said Navy Remington.

The monkey leapt from Remington's shoulder and was sitting in the passenger seat of the automobile before Fingo could open his dreading eyes. Several times he'd been threatened while sawing off a limb or yanking a molar. Even Judge Nitburg, amidst a migraine, had threatened him once. Poured near a quart of laudanum down the man, his patron, who had owned him for years since buying his degree and exonerating him from the matter of . . . eh . . . tenderness with an unhappy dying cowboy. But that was years, centuries ago, the Civil War still hot in the heads of the citizens and still some gray jackets on moochers and grifters. Remington spoke of new death — his. It was said Remington had beat off a whole pack of coyotes with nothing but a belaying pin.

— I think I'd better . . . need a punch, said Fingo, backing into the lobby of the hotel.

— He's still calling to you, holding up the money. That's my sister's boy, Fingo.

— I *have* to see a man about a horse.

Fernando suddenly spotted the automobile and his uncle on the veranda. He turned directly around and crutched back to the hovel.

My poor lad, stricken boy, thought Remington, though Fernando must be near forty by now. The wind's near blowing him over. Used to, the boy would dive off a cliff into the quarry pool and pretend drowning. Stay underwater a couple of entire minutes. Bobbing up a quarter of a mile away. Used to, he'd run down a tumbleweed in a full gale, jump over it. Slice it to bits with his bowie. Bring it home for kindling.

★

Smoot chose this range, all flat with a few joshuas and cactuses, to apply himself. He lay in the gulch with the enormous rifle, a Creedmore of the old buffalo school. He had shot it twice earlier. His shoulder was still numb and blue from the kick-back. But it had not knocked him over or embarrassed him, and the second shot took the head off a cactus fifty yards away. These legends like Buffalo Bill, he spat. Who could miss a beast with one of these cannons? This thing would stop an automobile. He wanted a still shot and not a mite scratched on the auto. So he had stolen a dress from Agnes Nitburg, some shoes, and a mannequin from Nell's Finery. It was a child mannequin that went with a mother mannequin, but they did not use it anymore as people thought it had false airs. So the mannequin child had lived in Smoot's fastidious room at the Nitburg Hotel, not out where the rabble could see, but in a closet, sometimes brought out when he took his supper upstairs and imagined an interesting guest from the East chuckling with him over the foibles of the herd. She had no name.

63

He was not insane or moon-lonesome. But he had written proverbs and epigrams all over her body in permanent black ink with a quill pen. She'd stood in his second pair of boots in the closet.

Before dawn she'd ridden with him through the dark and now stood out in the road in the dress, shoes and veil. That was correct, that was necessary. The road here crossed on top of a double arroyo. You had to move her or drive over her.

Smoot knew old Remington was close to deaf, which would aid Smoot in case the first blast did not take him. When he heard the car, however, he was painfully excited and moved fifty yards farther up the gulch. He trembled, the Creedmore becoming a ponderous thing. The monkey would be in the seat. What would it do? He was wild with tenderness for the animal. He could imagine nothing worse than her racing off across the plain without him. Wiping moisture from his eyes, he crept back farther into the gulch, losing most of his savvy. The automobile was really coming up and this would be no dream.

The car eased to, with a deep clicking. Half of it — Remington, the monkey and the yellow nose of the car with the white grille — was clear in his sights. Navy Remington (pompous, stuffed, unfortunate man, thought Smoot. Mr. Captain Navy Remington, grown so tall nobody could hardly miss him, Mister Seafarer with his buttons and pomp) and the Story of His Life and Times got a good ending to it now. This piece of work *evaporate* that thick book. He cleaned the front sight of the Creed-more with a wet finger. His tongue remained out in flat, mean concentration.

But he was shaken. Murder would put him onto another road entirely. That and the automobile and the monkey. They would be driving past a nature he had never seen before, nature coming at him fast in different shapes as never seen before. The wind and the wonderful eruption of the engine and the living things parting in front of you.

Remington walked to the mannequin in the road. He did not study it long before his seacap blew off. Curious, this, with little wind around. He fetched his cap some feet away, then came back to regard the dummy with the veil. He lifted the veil and there were things written all over its face. This was no ordinary scarecrow. "I highly agree!" read one of the lines. The dummy did a violent twist and fell to earth. This wasn't reasonable. Remington felt there was some oddness about. Why, the thing's foot had been powdered. This place was not right. He touched the stump of plaster. The shoe was nowhere to be seen. There was dreadful medicine going on here, perhaps voodoo. Kneeling in the road, he picked up the powder of the blown foot and read another line: "Fools rush in, ha ha!" Then the *head* of the thing was gone suddenly and he had sensed a popping of the air around him, something changed in the barometric. No head, no veil. Remington was frightened, in that part of him that had hardly ever been frightened before. Dust was in the air in front of him, just risen up like something spat from underground. He gathered the mannequin to him and rose with it. Then he walked slowly back to the automobile, looking all over the plain of joshuas and cactuses. But there was nothing. Maybe he was having an attack, a stroke, something cerebral. But he wanted the mannequin with him to prove he was not mad or fanciful.

Smoot was out of shells. His shoulder was broken. The monkey was leaping up and down in the auto seat, pointing Smoot's way and screaming. Smoot had sweat so much his hat had slipped down to his eyebrows, dragging his curls with it. He was furious at Remington, furthermore — if he could stand any more wrath — for taking the mannequin with him. *His* mannequin, his supper guest. This was terrible. This was unbearable. The thing had Smoot and Nitburg written all over it. Low . . . woesome . . . ignominious. Another new road indeed.

The automobile, the monkey, everything was gone. His whole right arm was gone. When he found the immense roan stallion, the thing peed on him. What else? He put his Saint Christopher medal in his mouth and wished he were already in hell. But provide me, Saint Man, with smooth travel there, he thought. Then prayed.

★

Obed Woods had tried to be a criminal in Nitburg for the last three months, but he was an addict of morphine and laudanum and the gang he was working with threw him out. They were petty thieves, but sometimes there was cash at Nell's Finery or Pete's Leather, and they would move in on it. They would not touch the Bank of Nitburg because of the time-lock safe. None of them had ever stolen more than sixty dollars at one time. There was only one little gun between them, and they were scared of that, because even Neb Lewton could shoot, and they couldn't. Dantly Lewton would shoot a dog just for practice, forty yards away. But even they kicked Obed out because he was such a mucker at his simple job, watching out for the Law — Neb and Dantly. Neb who barely got out of his chair but had killed a man thirty years before, and Dantly, his twin brother, who after nine o'clock at night shot first and asked questions *about where the bullet went.*

Obed would keel over on the ground from chemical fatigue, with coffee grounds all over his face. He ate coffee to kick him up but it didn't work. He would fall over yawning in the dust and Dantly would discover the break-in, every time, coming in with his pistol and noose. Judge Nitburg would send them to a lonely territorial prison so hideous and unreformed that the very structure collapsed periodically, releasing felons in all directions with bitter attitudes. Some came back to Nitburg and started the same thing all over again. But Obed was not among them. He was fired, even as a puny watch-out.

Fingo finally thought of him in light of Fernando, since Obed was now every day in his face, in his office, begging for morphine. He had brought his own syringe, but the doc was still standing off. The man was Black Irish from New York City and still had good-looking teeth and a wicked Irish grin that encouraged Fingo, the fairy, to give him five or six shots, though even in his comas Obed would never come across. He would curse Fingo and never even give him a niggardly toe to suck.

— Have you ever been *off* this stuff? Fingo asked him.

— Yeah. I been.

— What do you do?

— Woods reached for the doctor's throat and got only his shirt, dragging him forward to his own face with Fingo smelling of coffee and his last meal.

— Ya hoit, ya bastid! What else?

— But what do you do after that?

— Spanish-American War. For godsake, gimme da shot. Ain't you seen the wound in me balls?

— No. Could I?

— Shot foist.

— Now that you're fixed, I suppose there's no . . . testicle-showing?

— Lump it, goofer. Fill my jar, I be on my way.

— But it was mere water, Obed.

— Ya knowed if I had da strent I'd tear yer open.

— Settle down. I'm getting someone else over here. You'll like him. It's Fernando himself.

— Fernando Muré da hoofer and da boid?

— I can't understand this New York Irish gibberish.

— Gimme da injectionuh.

— Let me tie you in the seat with this little rope here . . .

Fingo went across the street and down to the wretched shack. The Chinese did not acknowledge him. Fernando was lying on the cot while little Stella, near death herself, stroked his forehead. She had tears in her eyes and was so concentrated on love for the man that she never heard the doctor enter. The place was lit by four sperm whale candles, and had the character of an enforced twilight.

— Is he eating anything? asked Fingo.

Stella looked up. — No. Nor I. We can't seem to need food.

He drew near the cot and placed his hand on Stella's shoulder. These people were so ill it touched even Fingo. An orchestra went off in his heart. Sympathy for the man with beautiful black-and-white hair spread out on the rotten pillow. Sympathy for the skinny hand of the woman who was stroking him. She couldn't even be a whore anymore. Since he could not touch Fernando he touched the woman. You could smell death itself coming off her, but his hand remained on her bony shoulder. It was the first time Fingo had really touched a woman. Another kind of music went through his hand. He had not expected the softness and mortality of her. Why, even *he* could break her in two and suck her face off as he would a crawfish.

Fernando smiled up at Fingo. — You brought me the relief, my man.

— Not this time, Fernando. We're getting you well.

Little Stella whispered up to Fingo:

— Me too?

— You too, Miss Stella, he lied.

— You goddamned pest. Get me a shot. I'll get some more money.

— Come along with me. Both of you.

When they left the hovel the Chinese were up and excited, seeing Fernando crutch along in a final way, Stella supporting him, coughing deeply, the doctor following with his hands behind his back.

The Chinese occupied the shack immediately. They had new relatives just come over for the bounty of America. There was a lot of cleaning up to do.

Obed Woods sat there withered and trembling, tied to his chair.

— What's going on here? asked Fernando.

— Mister Muré, would you take the other chair? I'm going to tie you up too, said Fingo.

He fetched a rope. Stella had drawn up the other chair in the office, sitting beside Fernando.

— Tie me up too, Doc, she said. — We'll get through this, Fernando. We'll get healthy, my man.

— Well . . . Fingo got a length of twine and tied her up.

They all sat around and looked at each other for

a while. Fingo was in a sort of paradise. He even desired this tubercular little *woman*.

— Er. Has anybody ever died ... *without* this stuff? asked Fingo.

Fernando looked at him dully.

Obed Woods spoke up:

— I don't know. I been on it since the Spanish-American War.

★

Shapiro, the solitary Jew in Nitburg, owned the other automobile and an eatery to the west side of the hotel. He was a clean man who eschewed almost everything, as far as the citizenry knew, except for his business and his Cuban woman. He ran his car just under the window of Smoot, black and blue and moaning with agony.

★

McCorkindale bought a fish at Shapiro's delicatessen. Fernando had been several days in Fingo's office room in the Nitburg Hotel. McCorkindale thought the man might like a toasted fish and some of that dark bread. Some radishes, too. Those were peppy-looking ones Shapiro had in there, big white ones that cheered the belly. Things were a bit relieved now for Reverend McCorkindale. He had never ceased praying, even in the narrowest valley of the shadow, when hair erupted in painful volleys. The hair had begun falling out, though, last week, with the warmer weather. He shed like a housecat, and his wereface reappeared as that of a stern Scotsman, blue eyes twinkling more than ever and his lips very red. The long black hair left his wrists and back, and he could feel more looseness in his thighs, which had really piled up with fur. His hips could now swing in his pants with a wonderful manly liberation, and he recalled his glorious days in that airplane. Shapiro did not know quite what the man was doing, standing around in the deli this long, approving of the food, sniffing and licking his lips.

— You need something else, Reverend?

— Just enjoying your store and my health, if you don't mind.

— Not at all.

— I like your automobile. What kind is that?

— That's a Ford. An open, plain Ford.

— I suppose you know . . . McCorkindale blushed, as he always did when he bragged, — I have flight experience.

— You can fly? asked Shapiro.

— I can. An old friend of mine has his own craft.

— How fast? How high?

— It's hard to remember, said McCorkindale.

Shapiro looked at him with a hard recollection. He'd seen only three aircraft in his life, and the men in them did not look like real human beings. He was certain that transmogrification occurred to those who were airborne. They were tiny friends with grins on them. McCorkindale, with his foolish gaze, did not look quite regular himself right now.

He was stunned by something way up there.

— Can I get you another mackerel, Reverend? asked Shapiro.

— Indeed, Mister Shapiro. My good man. Another.

★

She'd taught the children well. She rode straight into the hills that Friday with a pickax in the rifle scabbard, thinking about her one-room school, her pupils, all the littlest to the biggest. She was a good teacher and knew it fully. When she taught them reading, writing and arithmetic, she did it without a book for the most part because the Reader was beginning to bore her. The badminton with Agnes was an agony, the dominoes with the sluts was downright morbid, and clothes themselves were growing a bit tedious with nowhere really to go in them. Her father asked her to attend his trials, but the man was such a stiff little bitch in his judgments, which were long and room-emptying in their pedantry, illustrating hardly more than the tedium of Nature Itself outside the window, and he lost her. He liked to grab her and kiss her down to her teeth, however, at home.

— Step away, pony, she said to her horse.

There was something ruthless and circumspect at the same time about the judge — like a coyote on the lope. She held the locket once owned by Fernando's mother in her left hand, lifted it to her lips, and prayed for him. He had disappeared utterly.

73

Even McCorkindale would not say where he was. He might be at his old uncle's. The old man had not been to Nitburg lately. There must be something going on.

Nandina was smitten by nausea: she suddenly remembered neither where she was nor what she was doing. Her head's compass seemed to have fallen off. She was out in the wild counties and she could not remember what she'd lusted for. Her hands were unfamiliar and sweaty. Her throat and stomach wandered on her, pricked by a hot syrup of something like jalapeños. The weather itself seemed to have become curious. A blue norther coming in while the sun still shone. Over the ridge of the next hill something blue in the air like federal cavalry. And here it was Saint Patrick's Day. Moving in, with a blue dust above them, the snorting horses and sabers popping up like stars. Her mama's face formed from the blue dust and the silver above the cavalry.

Her lungs were full of hurtful dust. The cavalry had passed through her, over her, and here came the direct torment of the cold. The storm knocked her off the horse. Then the pickax in its scabbard whistled around and struck her in the back. She went black, and her head felt like it was crawling away on its own, lengthening her neck by yards and yards.

When she awoke she was hot. The sun was boiling her, and she raised up on all fours, spitting sand. Her long black hair was in her face. The big mesa to the east had a kind of fence on the top of it. Then she saw it was Indians, Indian horsemen, just staring at her in full feathers. The cavalry had run away from the Indians, and the Comanches had come up this close to her, just to stare and have their rifles, lances and purpose. She could hardly believe the skinny dark loneliness of the men on their horses. The war paint crossing and barring them, living in the air with wild purpose. Then wave after wave of men on horseback with the sharp edge of steel running through her head.

She was on her horse again, her back painful from the ax blow. She was having her first migraine and then she knew it — caught straight from the judge, her father, my damn! This was what they were like.

Randy Black, the very best pool player in Nitburg, was on a puny nag in front of her. He was scrubby in the cheeks and sunburnt after looking for a little gold along the creek. His pool cue and filter were tied on his back. This man could beat even Nermer, who was on the mountain now, the only man who'd ever possessed her.

Randy looked down at her with a sheepish grin. She was lying on the neck of her horse. Her head was now impossible with pain. Her right eye was shut. Tears were pouring from it. She cursed in a whisper. Was Randy all there was after the cavalry and the Indians and her mother appeared?

— You having trouble, Miss Nandina?
— Help me, please.

Randy got off the horse and stood beside her. He did not know whether he should touch her. She was one gorgeous thing, now she'd fallen off the horse again. She was on all fours weeping. Red ants were all over her arms.

— The ants are hurting you, he said and knelt beside her, handkerchief out. He flicked it at her sleeves. — You've fallen off on an anthill. Can you get up?

— I can't stand this, she said.

— You're covered with them.

There is absolutely no point to this pain, she thought, rising. Ants all over her, too, and a pickax bruise on her back. I haven't even done anything yet.

Randy gave her some water and she tried to look around the country. Even looking was painful. Her head began pounding with pain again while the rough man looked at her. She did not like to be seen hurting. But then, there was some relief to her head. The mesa beyond Randy was shivering, red and black, vacant. Now nothing was moving at all. The man with the pool cuestick on his back was smiling and offering an outstretched hand.

Nandina went frigid. Nothing was out here and the two of them were alone. It was not the right place to be, even with Black's hospitality. The pain had left her with the feeling of having been *occupied*. She was cold and empty.

— You been going through something, Miss Nandina, said Randy. — Like seen a lucination. It affected me and you and we come to a ground of common understanding.

— What are you talking about, Randy?

She dusted her knees with her hat, like a man.

— Seems some point me and you's alone on the golden plain. Like the onliest ones left on the earth and in my dreams of carrying on the race.

— You . . .

— I din't know how come I rode the lonesome plain so far from the streets, the roads, the houses, the crowd, everything I knowed as life except for a little gold in the creeks, and come upon your quietude like this, 'cept in a dream. Have you saw us together once before?

— You babbling ass.

— . . . fill our needs.

— You want me to *commit* something with you?

He got down on his knees.

She spat on him.

Then she got on her horse and urged it over the hill so Randy could not see her anymore. She rode past the great alkali lake. It was not much, but she owned *this* too, she thought. Out West, your eyes owned everything nobody wanted to possess. All these clouds and colors and distances, thank God. Nobody could get close to you. Not too close, like Nermer. She was glad he was up on the mountain, suffering. But eventually she would be in Austin, New Orleans, or Memphis, maybe San Antonio, where more people could look at her.

The Remington place was hers, too, she gloated

in the late afternoon. It lay down below her, a blond-logged U facing her, with the old man (his hair seemed longer and wilder, whiter) out dancing by himself. Not by himself but with a monkey that leapt straight off the earth when he came near, screeching, delighting him. Was he drunk? He was having too glorious a time here by himself with a mere animal.

She was a little envious.

I can change this, thought Nandina.

She rode her horse behind the barn and hid the pickax behind two bales next to the magnificent Winton Flyer, yellow and lusty with petroleum smells. The whole barn was a heaven of odor to her. She knelt and looked between the front tires where the earthen recession gleamed with oil. She put a finger underneath the car and sucked on it again. This was it, that lovely taste beyond everything. Her own sex tasted something like it, she thought. She'd always tasted like petroleum and the color of it was in her hair. Her brow was dripping with its taste.

Now. Now.

She soothed herself and went into straight, guileful avarice with her sex, her legs, her long youth, her brain, all she called her own.

Remington was holding the monkey and watching her with a wide smile when she rode down to him. He knew the schoolteacher very well. She'd come out once before, admiring his auto.

He had seen her dawdling in the door of the

schoolhouse with some hangdog older student who had some last remark to make before he could begin his dreams again. Remington was an old deaf connoisseur of women, though he had never married. His dreams were long, calm, expansive, very appreciative, what with the constant religious silence in between his ears. He'd never dreamt that he would be a dreamer, but now he was a good one. The pleasant harbors and the women, the lemurs and pumas hanging off limbs of the trees bordering uncharted small ports, smooth drums of the natives and the accordion under a pounding moon all orange at the equator.

★

Fernando, man, he said to himself. You with the broken knees, but now you can walk a little. Stella had improved with food and they sat out in the sun together near the old shack in a couple of hardbacked chairs among the busy Chinese. The Chinese were afraid he would want the shack back but he didn't, and had told them so. But he could not speak Chinese, and they looked at the pistol he wore now and they were troubled. But Fernando and Stella had a free room in the Nitburg Hotel by Doc Fingo and they were being mild. Fernando's legs seemed to have come to a better life around his kneecaps. They were surging with spark. He hardly needed anything but a cheroot and a meal now — and to polish his gun.

Stella still coughed, but she had put some more

flesh on her bones. She adored Fernando beyond earthly loves. They held hands in the sunshine. One of the Chinese would play the xylophone, and they listened to the pleasant wobbling chords falling from the window of the shack. Fernando would smile fondly and lick a bullet while the music hovered around them. Then they would go back to the hotel, hold hands, and fall asleep, clear in the head.

Fernando was dreaming of his factory, with the Chinese. He was among them and he had his factory, turning lead to gold, noisy and laboring, cursing, yelling with glee. He could not identify, quite, the real product yet, but it was wonderful and direly needed. His ambulation was intact. He rode a motorcycle, and overhead biplanes flew low and high celebrating his enterprise. Then he saw what it was — what the factory was. It was a coffin factory, the very finest of coffins of the best teak and mahogany, and he and the Chinese were shipping them out to New Orleans, San Antone, Austin, San Francisco, Seattle, New York, Chicago, Montana, Mobile. These coffins were prettier than new grand pianos. They were so beautiful that an elegy or sermon would be unnecessary. The people would see the coffins, and then McCorkindale and his planes would swoop down, and he would load one coffin onto a bigger plane and simply leave, delivering it to high heaven and then coming down, the big plane releasing the beautiful coffin like a pretty peaceful bomb into the blue ocean where his Uncle Remington had traveled. It would zoom like

lead to the bottom and come up flush among the
sea creatures.

★

Fernando saw Stella walk to Nell's Finery with fresh
dollars in her hand. This was part of his stake from
Navy Remington, who had posted the money to the
hotel. She wanted a hat and a dress, another size
now that she had gained weight. It was a sweet
thing with her well from consumption, oxygen in
her lungs and pink in her cheeks.

He remembered himself and his rifle in the City
of Mexico and his brain about the size of a shelled
walnut, out of fear. The air buzzed with bullets like
hornets. So many of them it was almost funny.

After that he had taken up the guitar just to have
something on his belly that would be hard to shoot
through. He knew he could not find the strings like
the greasers with the big hats did, and he knew he
could never be passionate on the instrument like
the violinist in Juarez, but he liked the big thing
around. It was something to hold on to.

★

The air was smart for enterprise. Nandina saw the
photographs of her father.

After making extreme love with old Navy Remington, with her washed hair down and her breasts
to his mouth and his surprising old thruster wanting more and more, with the monkey sitting there
calmly on the chiffarobe chewing on cashews and

silent as a tiny black and white god, the both of them went out to the barn and he backed up the Winton Flyer.

Nandina didn't speak for the rest of the day.

The monkey did not amuse her. She wouldn't eat. Old Remington, seduced and in ardor, felt altogether miserable himself. When he had collected himself from lust, he felt a puny man. Not even Fernando had seen the pictures. They really were too nasty to be witnessed and there seemed no great point to them now, except to break the heart of a daughter he had ravished. The judge's daughter, then the judge's pictures. It was a mean thing he was in, and he was not a mean man. But she had demanded and demanded to see his "secrets" and it was the first any woman had ever demanded anything at all from him. He loved the girl and her voice owned him. But this was wicked and small. Their sex had carried him over to unconscionable lewdness. This was life, this was blood, this was her.

The pictures had given him a bit of power, even rule, in the town of Nitburg. An aggrieved Confederate widow had thrust them on him before she died on his ship out of Galveston to Brazil. All that old honor, the Old Cause — it had been gone almost entirely a long time now. Remington looked out at his sheep near the river with the Mexican shepherds moving around in them. His life had been heavy with honor and duty, and he had never suspected that one afternoon with a naked woman could hurl him to depravity so quickly, within the day.

A man like him should never have had any such "secrets" at all, was the thing.

Broke a young schoolteacher's heart. He sincerely believed he had.

★

Fernando got drunk again. He didn't mean to, but he was sitting there on the hotel bed with a bottle on the dresser, looking between his knees. Stella wanted him to take coffee and food, but he wouldn't. He was not interested in the guitar either.

— Something in me ain't no captain of industry, Stella. Those coffins, that idea ain't me. I ain't got the cut for that. That was a damned moron thought. Fact is, I ain't been nothing at all and I been feeling too damned wonderful to do anything about it.

— But you've been nice, Nando. Real nice.

— Nice don't cut it for all of us. Nice could be a captured ape in a zoo.

— You could be a lot of things. Anything. Your uncle would help.

— Comes to the point where you ain't nothing but a couple of stories blowing around like a weed. You can't even keep none of your promises. And you're not even none of those stories anymore.

— But your testicles can really dance. I drew those little faces on them and you made them dance.

— That was just a relay from the guitar strings, Stella. Hardly any future in it either.

— Your hair is getting nice and silvery places, darling.

— Well I guess you just said it all to me pretty as a poem. A man has to stand up and do. I can't be just sitting here. Voices are calling me, dear Stella. Let's move.

★

Fernando set fire to the courthouse with a bottle of kerosene and then walked away with Stella in hand. It went up like a box of matches. Nermer saw it from the mountain and he stood up. He walked down the mountain very softly, seeing the fire, having nothing but his bare feet left. The fire came very close to the hotel, but an east wind blew it away. The magpies sat on Nermer's shoulders, and his little goats and armadillos wanted him, but he had to descend to the town, as he saw the black cloud of rain run by his left shoulder, onward and then down as if on a mission to extinguish the fire. He traveled more rapidly and his horny feet hurt when he reached the timber line, his little friends leaving him and loving him even after he'd eaten several of them. There against his hand was the big mama goat he'd always loved. She had lost her children and slept near him in the better cave that he finally went to when winter hit.

Nermer stepped more carefully. His feet were bleeding as he left his animal and bird friends behind. He was going back to a hell, but he wanted to see what happened and dwell with the fire.

And the minions that Nitburg had . . . Which building was it on fire? Which one was it that flamed so eloquently, popping the sky orange, crawled about by roving insect citizenry? He witnessed a storm roam right down in front of him — and what was this, coming practically over his ears? A biplane, with Reverend McCorkindale in the front seat and somebody else in the back. They were following the storm toward the fire. The storm was wandering down the mountain with rain above the fire and the hearkening folks. This must be what war is like, reckoned Nermer. Oh my feet, my feet. My dissolving rags. Be a raw nude John the Baptist sort of fellow when I finally make the town. As for the terror of those women of Lesbos in the back of the hotel in their well-known opium den, it must be intense by now, with the fire that close. Scrambling from the sin that knows no name, from the flames themselves, perhaps of hell, for kissing desperate others of their own kind.

Before the fire Nermer had never seen a lesbian up close, only heard they were there. He was anxious, though, to see one. Maybe assist one of the curious females to safer quarters. Maybe try some opium himself. Help, if he could, these forlorn sisters of the lesbianhood.

Nermer was hungry now for the town and all its sin. He was very homesick for sin. How he'd missed it, through his health and hermitness.

Did he hear shooting already?

Where was Fernando, who could really shoot and burn?

Nermer came down off the mountain and walked across a rocky meadow, near naked when the rotten cloth departed from him. He held his head up toward the dimmer orange of Nitburg with its sparks jumping at the moon. Only a belt of mule leather was left on him, and underwear made from his last bandana. He was a sunburnt thin man when he looked down at himself.

He walked past a high forest of cactuses, and then raced toward the smoldering buildings; Reverend McCorkindale flew overhead in the biplane, hollering down, "Nermer! Nermer! Back in town! Nermer is back in town!"

The plane came low and landed in the main street of Nitburg. The street was solid with four feet of dried mud, and the contraption put down violently with some serious leaning back and forth. It rolled earnestly toward the high and narrow church, wobbled, and stopped right in front of the smoking hotel. McCorkindale jumped out in his leather coat and goggles and long white scarf, another pilot following him.

They came toward Nermer and behind them ran out the tribe of distressed women in their frocks from the back of the hotel. Nermer shook McCorkindale's hand and received a great hug before recollecting his near nakedness, and bleeding. But smoke covered him, and after the Reverend hugged him, he looked into the billiards parlor where he had played eight-ball and acquitted himself well.

Then he saw Fernando dancing in the street. He was doing it with Stella as the piano went on, with the fiddles and cornet, along the crusted Main Street mud. Nermer thought she'd have passed on, but little Stella seemed healthy now. Nermer could barely believe it.

After the fire brigade formed, Nermer joined in the smoke, and helped the chain of townspeople hoist heavy buckets of water — mainly to save the pool hall and the hotel where he'd received his earthly reputation. He wore a long leather coat and a white scarf to block the smoke, a gift from McCorkindale, who was alongside him with the other pilot partner, trying to keep the fire away from the church.

But Fernando was dancing with Stella and laughing, eyes happy with reflected flames. It was rumored that the man could not only see behind his back but around corners.

★

Smoot hit the telegraph repeatedly to hire those that would shoot Fernando. Two weeks later, nine hired gunshooters came to Nitburg, and Smoot was armed with the same big Creedmore he had when he missed Navy Remington.

When Fernando burned the courthouse, he had made a great smoke in Smoot's room. Smoot had run from the hotel, horrified for his littleness. He was so low he almost ran underground, but he'd managed to get somebody else's horse, and race it into the desert, where a strange orange moon with smoke along its bottom edge trailed above him. Coyotes, seven of them, picked up his hot fear and ran after him and the horse for many miles. Smoot was practically elegant in his terror. He rode straight up and slowly so as not to fall off. The Creedmore was about to overturn him every second, and he was not used to the bay mare. One of these days soon, he swore as he rode slowly with the voracious beasts near his heels, the joke ain't going to be on me. An eternity rolled by before he came at last to the judge's house. The judge was on his front porch watching the orange sky to the east.

Even from this distance, two and a half miles away, they heard something extraordinary coming over the plat, echoes dying in the sand and the joshuas and the willows on the river behind the house.

It was the sound of a whole band, with drums and — what was this tinkling over the dunes? A xylophone. The band was not too wonderful but at the time, with the east wind taking it, the sound seemed to be coming up on the right and left very close to the house. The men on the porch armed themselves with what they had and the judge walked back inside.

Nitburg considered the fact that his daughter now had pictures of his treachery. She had seen her grandmother and her mother, both going away, though Nitburg had not thought of it in that fashion. Was he not on the great Lincoln's side in the first instance? It was a terrible war, brother against brother, hence child against mother. He was in the main sweep of an awesome history, and he could not help it. The wife Nancy Beech? You released wild things for their own good and yours too, didn't you? Wasn't it done? They "put away" wives in the Old Testament — it was ordained of the ancients. Nancy Beech had heard the rumor about his mother and laughed at him. She'd brought Nitburg no eminence, no lucre, no connection. Did not even know what an opera was, did not know what opera glasses were, yet had to fall in heat for the first tenor of the first opera through the first society binoculars she'd . . . had to fall in heat, a rabid despondency of lust over a florid pompadoured dago keening over a dead woman on the floor of a stage in New Orleans. Just about ate up the flowers between herself and the strutting fool in the dressing room. Wanted the privileges later and she lifted up her skirt, spread herself all cockeyed with champagne, all moist for another man, called out to him "Sing for your supper!" Sure, she was trash, and he'd have let that one go because of the champagne and the sudden high society, but there was the other matter of, well, it was the final punch on her ticket to Indianland, that thing, that habit of poverty she had that mortified his . . . that, just . . . was *it*. She poured honey on ham fat and ate it, right in front of the governor. She liked animals too well, even chickens. She'd had that provoking far-off gaze out the window ever since the opera wetness, spying out some repulsive dream land, some ungrateful foreign wretchedness. Well, there was a land for her, all right, and contacts were made all right, and she fetched a bit of gold when her dreams came true all right. Though the singing and the hooting might be a little rawer than what her damned loony eyes were looking for. Sing for my supper, sure.

He got in the bathtub running the cold water over his hot feet. Finally, he could not hear the music anymore, and knew no infantry or cavalry had come to attack him. From his tub of Vermont marble he could hear the new hired men stepping around the grounds, talking mildly, and he was more at ease. The pain never even came close to his temples.

But then his wife Agnes opened the bathroom door and stood there with her cane, her long white dress, and her hair to the floor around her bare feet. Charlotte Agnes Dunning, a stunning square-jawed society millionaire in San Antonio with her newly dead husband when Nitburg met her — some hair left on his head and with a stealthy charm, also with a river of silver-tongued words flowing from the pool of law around him: the torts, the precedents, the clean law, as a rabbi might have bathed in. When Nitburg took her for his bride, the yellow fever was on and he collected a great many cheap army barracks near Austin with help from the governor. Partitioned, they rented well to the likes of impoverished Confederate widows, amputees and itinerants, half of them alcoholics and addicts whose needs were attended to at the "town" store, which sold whiskey and army morphine with a few beans and some salt pork up front. Nitburg became deft at attaching pensions and inheritances through credit and carrying charges, and there was a happy rotation of the dead and the mad hauled off the premises by healthier alcoholics who worked for him. All of it executed by crystalline law. The remaining orphans he sold outright to various gold rushers heading west. These were "apprenticeships" with finder's fee, clear as a bell. Of the wife seventeen years his senior, what could be better? Who was the fool who prescribed passion for marriage, with its drool and jealousies? Why, even his stiff chilliness seemed to attract this woman, whose husband had died crazed and syphilitic.

There was the one matter of the large son in the carriage with them that Sunday afternoon as Nitburg rode the precincts in his single demonstration of Rollingwood Barracks to Agnes. An old morphined haint of a vet leaned out of a window and vomited.

— Something's not right here, somehow, said Agnes.

— Duly noted from the henhouse, Nitburg said before he knew it.

The big son stopped the carriage. — Just a minute. Come around here, Mister Nitburg. They went behind the carriage. — See here, spoke the son, and popped him square in the face. He sprawled and sat up dusty-backed.

— That wasn't pleasant, that 'henhouse' thing. I believe we are looking largely at my mother's money.

— Duly noted, muttered the ringing Nitburg. (His head had not been right since.)

That and that damned meddling fool Charles Dickens, who came to Austin, read in the theater, and denounced Rollingwood from the stage. Snot-bearded limey poking around our America. Brought to shore in Galveston by Navy Remington himself, they said. With those damned photographs.

Two months later Agnes had a stroke that took her eyes away and crippled her on the left.

He promised her her own whole town. With his earnest, knitted brow he traced the Colorado River to a hamlet far west and harvested the dot with his eyes. There would be no operas and no theaters there. Even the map seemed barely interested in the place, blurring out. There could be certain strokes welcome there. He had heard rumors of enterprise there, real enterprise.

By then his daughter Nandina was budding. He was thrown into an entranced felicity with the young beauty, in whom he believed he saw the lineaments of a grace denied him by rough western history.

Their Mexican woman taught old Agnes to hit

the birdie and play it back in a game called badminton while Nitburg calculated the map and began populating it. The first arrivals were Doc Fingo and Edwin Smoot, who had become handy at Rollingwood Barracks. There were others who came along solely because of the morphine, a rolling young fortune unto itself. While he was at the map, he touched himself and exuded a pleasant sweat. Here was real creation. Here was enterprise.

But here was Agnes standing in his own bathroom with her cane and her long hair, tamping on the ground, saying:

— Kyle, I hear such fortunate music. There were sounds in the air more lovely than a bird's singing. It was a band, a whole band. Dear Kyle, what, God damn it, does the world look like? Tell me.

— Go away, Agnes, I'm naked. There could be violence. There could be strangers with guns nearby.

— I smell something wild, something burning.

— From here? What you smell is the hitch. The knot in things. Seems like there always has to be one.

He was wishing his daughter was here right now, so he could kiss her, right down to the teeth. Outside his window, in the east, the sky was lowering from orange to yellow.

— Actually, it's rather pretty out there, he said. It makes me sleepy somehow.

Nitburg saw three hats and faces on a ridge, several guns with them.

93

— We have us a land here, really, where no heroes are required.

— I used to be somebody, said Agnes. — I was something with a smile. I liked smooth things, sarsaparilla ice cream, my spring carriage, raw cotton. Now I've got this block of dark to walk around in. He put out my light and . . . I've truly loved only the music of the church and the voice of that young man . . . Fernando.

— He's really not required. They have the radio now, Agnes. I doubt the man is anything. Doubt he has one dream that'd square with the earth. Best go on now and get a haircomb from Juanita.

Edwin Smoot stood all dusty and haggard out in the hall behind Agnes.

She could smell his gamy presence and moved backward to her large windy room with the curtains whipping out blond with lilac flowers printed on them. She knew the house very well now. Smoot was a piece of low smoke in it. She found her bed and the cool air and strained her ears for the music.

Smoot came in while the judge was wrapping up in his robe. The judge was sweating all over again. He knew the dwarf's mouth was full of trouble and for a brief moment he had a superfluous urge to hang Smoot. The man did not go with the room they were in now, the study, crowded with law books black and gold and red. Nitburg had saved robes from presiding at the bench over the years, and they hung stiff with officious sweat on the walls. The bought men, either swaybacked, potbellied or consumptive, milled into the study. There were two real sharpshooters, gumming away about Tom Horn and Geronimo, but Nitburg blanched when he saw them. They were as old as Agnes. Among them, the group had been shot one hundred and nine times. One came in late and meekly, trailing dog excrement.

— You have a lot of dogs, your worship. Could I possess one?

Nitburg looked at him blankly. A pre-senile boy of some sort.

— They're my daughter's.

— I'm Snuffy. Could I possess your daughter? The boy was squirrelly, about exactly the size of the ten-gauge he carried.

Somebody cuffed him.

— Could we get a designated leader here? asked Nitburg. — I'll be using English. Perhaps an *interpreter*, then?

— Pet's the meanest, came a voice from the back. — He hollowed out a Spaniard and wore him to escape.

— I been in every modern war, said a tall man in a coyote parka. — Spanish-American, World War One, World War Two.

— That ain't been held yet, clicked Smoot. They looked down toward the front. — What's wrong with *me*? I know the layout.

— Old friend, smiled Nitburg. — I was . . . praying for a bit more . . . no, *less* subtle —

— I can listen, I can lead, I can shoot, spoke out

a jowly man in an old cavalry jacket with chevrons on the sleeve. He was in the middle of the group but his low barbed growl made a path. He stepped forward and took a long pipe from his mouth. White hairs were on his chest where his longjohns parted.

— Done. We have here ... men ... a pest. Nitburg held the giant decanter on the desk and at last splashed himself a vast toddy as he spoke. The group hearkened to him with blind thirst. — The effect of my life, this struggle on the darkling plain, has been creation, quite from practically nothing, I might add. Men, like me or not, you are staring at civilization. Fate has prepared me, and I am a special kind. When there was nothing and then there is something, whatever that is, is right. When there is nothing to eat and then there is something to eat, that is good. Gentlemen, I am the last water in the well. Not so tasty, perhaps, but water, and it is right.

The judge yanked on the decanter and served himself another tall one.

— I deputize you, he said.

— Kneel, kneel! cried the man of all wars.

— This ain't the goddamn middle ages, clicked Smoot.

Nitburg, enchanted by whiskey and the moment, opened his desk drawer and withdrew a four-barreled thirty-eight derringer, a thing of handsome golden snouts pulled off a bankrupt drunken gambler by Neb Lewton years ago. He raised the weapon above his head.

— I shall not be moved!

★

The rest had gone out. Smoot remained, chewing a soda cracker. Luther Nix, the chevroned deserter, herded the men toward the hitching post and refilled his pipe, looking at the peppered moon.

— This ain't much, he said. — Really, there's too many of us. Meaner, leaner's what we need. Come here, Snuffy, that your name?

Snuffy came up with his giant ten-gauge. He was a very dirty little man with raw red gums like a wound amongst hair. The crowd knew something was up and stepped away.

— Kill yourself, said Luther Nix, without taking the pipe out of his mouth.

Snuffy stared at him and grinned.

— Say? I ain't possessing your sense.

— I said put that goosegun in your mouth and blow your head off. We got a population problem here.

— You mean . . . Snuffy brought up the gun, shifting as if he didn't want it anymore.

Luther Nix raised the forty-four Colt from his belt and shot him in the stomach. The pipe stayed clenched in his teeth. Snuffy staggered back with huge eyes and reached behind him where his colon was blown out the back. Then he spiraled and fell.

97

The others made a great clatter receding from the explosion and the body.

— This man have any friends? asked Luther around.

Nobody said a word. They were paralyzed with awe, and saw Snuffy standing and alive a second before, saw him over and over, then saw him on the ground moaning.

— Why, I think little darling is still alive. Are we now, little darling? Well . . .

Luther Nix brought out a long flash of steel from his hip and knelt, seeming to wrestle vaguely a bit and then snapping something as the man on the ground gurgled. Nix's hand chopped down, and then he arose with the head held high and streaming against the moon. The men could not believe it and roamed close to take stock. It was as if a man had performed magic on a stage somewhere. He was so busy with the head they felt safer.

The ponderous thing was that they knew he had done this *before*.

— We'll let darling Snuffy be lookout, then, said Nix.

He jammed the head on a picket of the fence near the hitching post.

— You. He hardly paused, beckoning the man called Pet, who was scared white. — Ride into town and witness, my angel.

— Witness, sir?

— Just relay what you've seen Mister Muré's way.

Nitburg and Smoot had come out when they

heard the muffled gun blast. Nitburg was transfixed to the head on his fence. He did not know what it was and sent Smoot ahead. Everybody was just standing quietly by then. Luther Nix was relighting his pipe. Smoot came back after a long minute. He was beaming with admiration.

— Nix is your man, sir. He has foresight. They watched the single rider trot his horse east toward the town. That would be Pet, the supposed hard one, and he was merely a messenger.

★

— Smoot, asked Nitburg, trembling, — am I truly corrupt?

— Of course, sir. The Meecham bribe, the Holst bribe, the Chancellor blackmail, the Chinese deeds fraud.

— Yet Nitburg *is*, is it not?

— The town?

— Am I seeing a little gray in your hair? What did we have when we first came twenty years ago?

— Nothing. A man selling water.

— And what happened to him?

— I poisoned him, per your instructions.

— But slowly, wasn't it?

— Yeah. Slowly, with Fingo's stuff.

— You know something, friend Smoot?

— What, sir?

— It's Christmas Eve.

★

99

One of the hired gunmen at the Nitburg house wasn't a hired gunman. In the study he mingled toward the back, staring ahead fiercely through wire-framed glasses. He had a scholarly look and whispered about the long ride from Colorado, but in fact he was Obed Woods, reformed morphine addict and a friend of Fernando's. His disguise required bare stealth, because the dwarf had never seen him healthy and Nitburg had never seen him at all. He was sweating terribly, however, and he had not thought even to bring a gun, any weapon at all. Woods had not shot a gun since Cuba, and to his memory had never done one good thing in his life. This was his maiden good thing, and the terror was awful. It surpassed the wound in Cuba when he was eighteen. He did not have love of his country then. He had love of Fernando, but this was a sweaty thing. His clothes were drenched and his veins were way out on his head.

Outside, with Nix and the explosion and the head, he was already on his horse and near fainted. The horse caught his fear, smelled the blood of Snuffy, and headed back to town while Nix was instructing the man called Pet. Woods was down the road, expecting a shout or a slug from Nix the whole first mile. Then he expected to be ridden down by Pet, who was a vicious hero in the very war in which he himself was a coward, pissing and moaning about his butt wound.

But he reached Fernando a good thirty minutes before Pet appeared, just after dawn in the hotel dining room. The place was acrid from the nearby fire. Only Stella, then, was sitting there at a table, drinking water, staring out at the sleeping hogs in the ruts of the street.

Pet walked over to her. By now he had reestablished his dignity and highly resented being Nix's mere envoy. He intended to kill Fernando himself and then Nix too if it came to it. He had almost forgotten for a while what a fierce and vicious person he was.

Stella had become almost plump. Though her lungs were still very weak, her bosom had swelled, and she was a remarkable creature in the gray dawn, drinking water in the smoky hotel.

Pet Rankin was hungry, violent and sexually aroused. Only a farm woman or a whore would be up at this hour and this wasn't a farm woman.

— You know a Mister Muré? Rankin said, seating himself right before her face.

— Somewhat.

— I hear the man likes a fire. I hear he's got the Chinee with him.

— I hear he's very sick. After the fire he got very sick. Went up to the mountain, very scared and sick.

— Not much of a finisher, huh. When'll he be back, reckon?

— I never seen him sick like that.

— You know him fairly well? I believe he will be sicker when you tell him that Luther N— He stopped and considered. — Some nonadmirers of

Fernando Muré got restless last night, shot and tore a hillbilly's head off. And he was on *their* side.

Stella looked down at her water and bit her lip.

— That's a dreadful rough crowd you run with, mister.

— Pet Rankin. Lately of Matamoros and the Glick Riders. 'Ninety-eight, I myself while in Cuba was obliged to gut a Spaniard and drape him across me, walked right out of their lines.

— Oh no.

— The man was alive, I hesitate to say before a morning blossom of your charms. I'd like to gut the person put a knife scar to your face, though it ain't really that bad.

— You're so extra rough.

— I've been a long time on the trail, if you catch my drift. He flared his nostrils and cocked his hairy eyebrows.

— I'm duty-bound to tell you I got the clap, sir.

— Well then . . . A pity. Looks like back to the ranch. You remember me and the headless man to Mister Muré. I'll bet he likes a good story. I'll be gettin' my feed and water from the Chinee and telling them too. This ain't somethin' they'd want to miss out on.

— How you hold yourself, it'd take a tiger to tame you, sir.

— Shh — He lit up, near to explode with worth and danger. Then he left.

Within an hour he was back on the rideway to the judge's, whistling bits of a hopeless love tune. "Oh, sir, my big, big tiger! Oh my, sir! Oh my horseman, dear sir, on! on!" he began saying suddenly in a little girl's voice.

He'd gone half a mile on the flats when he heard someone calling. He turned in the saddle and saw some blamed fool running out of the buildings and down into a dip, then up onto the flats again, veering into the rideway, like a deeply sincere and anguished sprinter. The man was really churning, as if something were behind him, but Rankin could see nobody following.

Fifty yards away he saw the man had closed eyes. The man seemed in great pain and urgency.

— Wait, wait!

— Wh— His horse stood quiet. This lunatic was near sprawling, kicking dust behind. His hat was in his hand. He staggered in the last wretched yards, panting and weaving ghastly. When he got near Rankin's horse he lowered his head and leaned on his legs, seeming close to vomiting.

— I thought, never, almost, near . . . to. The terror. The stark fear. It doesn't seem fair. My awful God.

He raised up and Rankin saw something wrong in his face. He was speaking smoothly and didn't seem that blown.

The man threw his hat down. He began stomping on it and raving.

— These old hats is so heavy, so heavy! The man thrashed his black and ashy hair.

Then he pulled something from the back of his

pants and shot Rankin swiftly in both shoulders. By the time Rankin's arms were blown back, palms up, the man had grabbed the bridle and pushed the muzzle of the gun deep in Rankin's stomach. He followed the panicked horse around as if glued to Rankin's belly.

— Please stop the horse. I'm scared to death and I might kill you. The man was not pretending now. Rankin kneed the horse in.

— I guess you'd be Fernando, damn you, said Rankin.

— I didn't want to be this much Fernando. You know, you start with little things, they grow, pretty soon there's something grown beside you looks like you. Get on, I'm damned crazy in the head.

The horse turned toward the Nitburg house. Fernando watched them a while, until the rideway lowered them — Rankin wobbling like a dummy atop — and his eyes blanked out on a spooky heat shimmer.

Then Fernando fell to his knees and wept, wild grieving sobs, right in the hot rideway.

★

Rankin held on with his desperate knees and bridled punily with his hands. You weren't supposed to have a man run out of a town like that and plug you, there wasn't any reason in that. And he had just sat there like waiting for a letter. Monstrous poor luck. But the man hadn't killed him. He didn't understand that. That was better luck. Fernando should've killed him. Only he sort of acted like a man dead already, that Fernando. In a way he was odder than Nix. The nerves were coming back now and he was in a grievous state. The horse could not step softly enough for his shoulders.

The entire morning had been odd, too odd, and you put that with his lack of sleep and it was nigh a dream. The woman alone in the hotel dining room where a whore shouldn't be, the smell of smoke and the charred courthouse with the cage of the jail still standing unburnt in the rear. Nobody else. Not a sign of Chinee, though their shanties connected by clotheslines were there. He might have shot a Chinee just for sport. Those sleeping hogs in the ruts were not right either. Something damned sickening in that.

It's taking a year, he thought, and I'm going the wrong way. They all knew about the fortune in morphine in the bank vault. The dwarf had bragged about it. Maybe there was some at the house.

Finally the house came into view; men were gathered around outside, and his heart went down suddenly when he saw something hanging from the tree. He felt very old and dry and gray. Both of his arms were liquid. The amount of blood on his stomach and saddle was enormous. Then he saw they had slaughtered a steer. They were having breakfast. Some old Mexican thing was helping them with a great pot of coffee over a fire and it did smell fine. Rankin was violently thirsty. He had not been able to raise his canteen. The men parted and there was Luther Nix, kneeling with a stick and a piece of hot meat on a knife half a yard long, it seemed.

— Ho, man! Oh it's my angel. You ride weird, old lonesome.

— I've been shot-up bad, Mister Nix.

— Why, the boys and me're just having Christmas, ain't we, boys?

— Yes sir, they all said.

— This is Christmas? asked Pet Rankin.

— Somebody plucked you right on Christmas day. Who was this person?

— Fernando Muré himself. If I could have some help getting off. One of the ancient scouts and a man with a sad walrus mustache and bald head edged toward the horse.

— Wait, wait. Hold on. We need more testimony here. We need some reconnaisance. What of the town, my angel?

The dread in Rankin had swarmed him like a coat of ice. His heart fell deep and nowhere. He looked over at the picket fence with the corner of his eye. The head was still there, swarming with flies. He was extremely cold. He was in his own personal weather, looking out of a hard terrible fog at the rest of the men. He looked around for helpful eyes but couldn't find them.

— There were just the hogs and the one woman. A whore drinking water. I delivered the news. This Muré run out and shot me. I thought he was crazy.

— I heard the man was hardly anything but a drunk and an acrobat with a good singing voice, spoke Nix. He was still chewing on the beef and the smoke from it came out of his mouth.

— He tricked me.

— Eh. Figure that.

Nix flared his coat with his elbow while the knife with the meat flew up in the air. His right arm seemed to be very much longer for a second, but it was the Colt and he blew Rankin out of the saddle with three rapid shots, the last one through the top of his forehead. Rankin turned a slow back somersault off the horse's withers and plopped flat supine on the ground.

— Trick is, said Nix as if he'd just escaped a huge jeopardy, — your eye picks out those fingers inching toward the butt of that short-gun a good piece of time before that even ever happens. Sometimes, an *hour* before. Nix let blow a roaring broken giggle.

— God rest ye, merry gentleman. He made a *poot* sound with his lips and stooped for his knife.

The men crouched back down. One had fallen in the fire and knocked over the coffee. He tried to set the pot back up as if this mattered. His hands were burned but he could not emit a noise. He just tried and tried again to get the pot right on the grill.

Then there was a long, long silence.

There were very careful murmurs then. Things like "ain't remainding many of us left, this keeps on." Or so Nix thought he heard. He looked over at the ancient scout, the man from Geronimo and Horn adventures. ". . . thinned out," the old man finished.

— Not at all, Gabby. We ain't thin *enough*.

— I didn't say nothin'.

— You bet you didn't. Say, Gabby, you're an old man. You don't look like nought but a stick with a mouth-hole. It ain't even apparent where you shit.

The leathery old fellow was shaking and gulping, about to relieve himself unwillingly.

— That Geronimo, he couldn't even see you coming, could he? But . . . Maybe you're too old. Ever consider that? You ever of a morning, say like this fresh Christmas morning, with the judge inside sucking his turkey and that old lady farting cranberries, think about blowing your head off? Just so there wouldn't be so much upright shit on the world?

— I been nicked, nicked, nicked twelve times, sir, tried Gabby. — I am old, but I'm mean, mean, mean, too.

— You just a smelly old echo, coot. But I seem to like you.

Gabby smiled broadly. They all relaxed. Some remembered they had never noticed Nix replace the Colt, but it was gone. It was very chilly and they loved it when Nix buttoned his coat. Something blue and northern was blowing in.

— Now, Gabby. You and some of the muckers cook his fingers up and eat them. That's right, Rankin's. Just about one apiece. Tasty.

— Rankin, Rankin, Rankin? asked Gabby.

— No quitters, said Nix.

He walked to the tree, threw a blanket over himself, and slept the entire day.

Smoot had observed it all from the shadow of the buggy shed. Two men got silently on horses and rode away, just disappeared without a word. The others hacked off, fried, and ate Rankin's fingers very quietly at the end of the day when the sun fell down.

What a man, Nix, Smoot thought. He's done this *before*.

★

The plane lifted and strolled in the air. It was exceedingly cold up there. They blew around in the wind as if direction of any sort was out of the question, then the propeller seemed to chop into something a little more solid and certain. They wavered off to the eastern counties and Fernando was thrown hard against the right fuselage. He felt very modern, too modern, loony. He was not there, he was so modern. Somebody else alongside him had occupied this big raccoon coat and was there. The man in back flying was named Python or Tiger, he couldn't remember. Pilot friend of the Reverend's. Flew for oilmen. What could an oilman be like, climbing down in a hole until he fell in it? Never saw the sun, stayed pitch black and sullen like a tar baby forever? How could an airplane help him?

Fernando was stricken terribly by an awful thing, beyond the chattering of his teeth: he was dumb. He was immutably stupid. The terrible loneliness of this knocking cold craft proved it. His college did not mean anything — it was another cold airplane in the sky wobbling toward nothing. A blessed man might go through life assured that he was everything but stupid, maybe scrambling for quarters in a saloon but not stupid. This low revelation brought tears to his eyes. The prison days, the Mexican adventures, the accident of the three shotgunners, the murdered drunken hours, months, years. His imprecations and his sulks, his painful kneecaps, the dwarf Smoot still running free and with a nest egg, no doubt. But Fernando had no stash, no hump, no scratch, no booty, no cache, no hand. His singing voice went out, his stupid dream of a coffin factory went out — why, it was just no better than the dirtdumb song of all Mexico. Some fornicator without even a bicycle crooning away about why the queen don't adore him. The Chinese liked him, sure, because he was idle and cruel, while they scrabbled for belly lint. Must remind them of some old tyrant back home. Bunch of them dumped off the end of a railroad spur, nobody told them. Nitburg taxed them for their hog space. That and the opium. (Those Chinese got pregnant quiet and quick. Seemed like there was a new nub in a bundle every three weeks.) Nitburg tossed some drifter in the jail for nothing, thirty days, introduced him to opium, had a lifetime customer and slave. (Why did Nitburg *need* so much? Why was there a moat-wide hunk of business all around him? Because it was there for the taking and nobody else saw it and he was smart? Because he was queer for a buck? Because he relished people like Fernando paying Nitburg to be Fernando so Nitburg could be Nitburg? he thought dumbly.)

He could not make the Chinese understand his feelings about the airplane, but he knew they'd seen him frightened. They did not realize it was fear of the plane, abject and pure. Smiling at his gestures, they had probably thought he was going hunting.

The pilot called up to him. — Look down!

— I don't really want to! he shouted back, hunched.

— No! I mean look down! Is that it!?

Fernando peered over the edge. A vast herd of sheep with tiny Mexicans in it. Then the barn with the Winton Flyer in it, curled spangling river to the right.

— That's it! Yes! Fernando was near sick and then the craft goosed up suddenly, banked right in a lost motion full of woe, it seemed to him, everything groaning and near collapse, wires popping.

★

"They're still there," said Remington. Nandina was holding the monkey and acting familiar around the quarters. Fernando did not quite comprehend the air here. She had good legs on her and they were propped on an ottoman rather smugly, a little cheroot smoking in a tray beside her on the couch. Yet she looked grim and weary.

And the old man looked shy. He looked fresh. He had the slight jitters.

— With ammunition too, yes. Not a lot. They're old Navy Spencers I got a deal on. Practically historical now.

— They could save my life.

— Why don't you just leave, my boy? Keep flying and flying. You've the contraption that was made for it.

— Certain . . . things are committed. Men have gathered.

The old fellow twisted his mouth. He himself felt he had gone over the bridge in showing the pictures to Nandina. He was an old, seduced fool. It was low business. It was unworthy. It was nasty as Nitburg himself. He was a vile fool on the rut. The last wild horses of himself had dragged photographed muck from him.

— Give him the guns, Navy, said Nandina. — My grandmama and my mama say so.

Fernando did not know what this could mean. He considered Nandina again, out here cozy and queenly, stroking the monkey. It was stroking the monkey most of all. She was a lengthy regent in her chamois riding habit, and his stomach stirred despite his despair.

— Who would shoot them?

— Some friends . . . with some Chinese.

— Chinese? Why would the Chinese shoot?

— They adore me. And they're starving. And I will pay, I hope. That money you said was mine in the barn.

— My boy. True. But I had hoped for some, say, enterprise.

— I ain't a boy, Uncle Navy. I'm near a dead idiot.

— I'll go to the barn with him, said Nandina.

Old Remington blushed.

At the barn Nandina backed out the Winton Flyer and showed Fernando the pickax. The soil was already loose, and he stared at her. She had come alive again. Her eyes were bright and mean.

— There's lots down there. Guns, money, pictures.

She closed a door of the barn. He began digging. The sweat and the fear leapt on him. He could not remember physical labor. It was a hateful thing. Pounding away at your own slot in the ground, some god behind the door busting his ribs to keep in the laugh.

— You came out of the air. You smell like the air and gas, said Nandina.

He could not help it, he began crying, mildly at first but then with disguised heaves as he went into the ground. He kept his head down. His hair fell forward.

— Men complicate a little thing like this, she said.

He heard a rustling between the falls of the pickax. Next, he looked right and saw her bare from the waist down, sitting on a bale of hay. Her feet with boots off were white as the moon.

— You take a look at those pictures. Then you kill my father. You leave me enough for an automobile. Navy promised me that.

— But Stella . . .

— No, you're just *with* Stella. Ever since you saw me, it's me you want. You might as well know I'm something of an alley cat and I don't care.

After the airplane was still, the propeller idled, in Nitburg, Fernando spoke to the pilot, Python Weems.

— What was the World War like?

— Loud, said Weems.

— You don't mind old gold, do you?

— Anything that spends. You seen that nitro blow them sheep up?

— Yes I did.

— It was old but it worked.

★

Luther Nix was gone in the night. Gabby spied over and he wasn't there anymore, just his blanket. He did not need them at all and he was in Nitburg doing the task of Fernando by himself, is what Gabby and the others thought for a long while. They were frozen and they ganged near the fire and commenced squabbling. Nothing was proven except a general weak anger, which they lobbed back and forth for over an hour. The man of all wars asserted himself, but they knew he was a lunatic. He wore himself out and soon all of them cursed, fell around the fire, and dove into a profane sleep.

Somebody put a hand on Gabby's shoulder and drew him up, then pushed his head down, snatching his rump up in the air. Then it was cold on his privates. Something had slashed his pants and he was butt-up, eating dirt. Then a fantastic pain entered his rear. Before that, he had felt spitting and blowing on his nethers, but now the pain indescribable.

— Wawwwww! he spoke. His head was pushed down, lips flat in thin garlicky grass.

— Shhhh! old Gab. Told you I liked you. It was the low whisper of Luther Nix.

Smoot was sleeping with the hirelings by now, and he raised his head, groggy and alarmed. In the twilight edge of the fire, he saw the shadow of Nix moving back and forth over Gabby.

Nix might have seen him watching. Smoot was the only one awake. The whisper was louder, and carried over to him.

— Guess that's about all there is. Money and sex. And grit, said Nix.

Nix never stopped hunching, bleakly and almost sorrowfully, Smoot thought.

— Piece of history here, old Gab.

Smoot closed his eyes, straining at the lids, but opened them helplessly again.

— Them fellows were riding off with some un-earned money. He was idly yanking Gabby back and forth now. — But there was a part of them that wanted to come back.

Smoot understood something hard and possible at the very edge of the fire closest to him. It was quite possible that those were the heads of the two who had ridden off earlier.

— Nothin's really that strange, whispered Nix, who was near his crisis. — I heard that someplace niggers have their own newspaper.

Earlier in the night, Agnes heard something at the cracked window beside her bed. It was a singing, weeping sound. It came in with an awful odor from the yard, something dead and rudely decaying. The little singing and weeping sound seemed to come in on a frowning breath of human rot, sweet and keen. The notes and sobs, on the other hand, were pathetic. A trapped voice in an odor.

She recognized it.

Somebody was just under her window, huddled, mewling. Yet there was haunting goodness in the voice.

— Fernando Muré?

— Quiet, Mrs. Nitburg. I'm stark raving. I'm not even here. God help me.

— Nor I here, my child. What is the world like? What's happening?

But he was already gone.

Nitburg was sitting with his knees on the couch

in the front receiving room, holding a curtain to the side and peering at the head on the fence between him and the fire of the bought men. He did not have the courage to ask Nix to take it down.

Nix could make nothing from something so quick, as he could make something from nothing in not much time. Perhaps they were bound to meet.

Having announced this symmetry, he lay down and slept like a baby.

★

— I seen a coolie with a gun, said Dantly Lewton. — He darted right back in his shack, but he had a gun all right.

— I was in the building when it burnt up, you know, said Neb, the other sheriff. They were standing in the charcoal in front of the cage of the jail. — My damned old hat caught fire, and before you knew it, why, I was concerned.

— The Chinee is a interesting nation. Before they was discovered it's purported they weren't yellow at all. But being discovered made them mad and sick.

— I required just three things from a woman: her hair combed, her mouth shut, and her legs spread. Wish I'd ever had one. I've never even had a pal, except you, who was my twin, and that was more like just two of the same liking nothing.

— Every Chinee is a twin.

— My eyes water when I think of having one

whopping huge meal and then cutting my throat. The good Lord above give so many golden opportunities for suicide, and what'd I do? Wasn't up to 'em, let 'em pass. Sorry, shh. They ought to hang me.

— Marco Polo knocked a hole in that wall and they come spilling out madder'n hornets. Don't believe in eating. Confusionism.

— Thing is, I never *worked* toward suicide. Fernando, how I admire that man, God give him a few talents and he didn't hide them under a bushel like me, not at all. He went after it. The rest of us just shuffle and wait, and before you know it, what, shit, natural causes, another dumb casualty, with so much promise.

— I seen Fernando swimming naked in the cold river this morning.

— Glorious.

— He's not right. Weeping and singing sometimes.

— He's perfect. Just at the age when there's nothing really left. The lumination comes early to a lucky few.

— Ain't even drunk. That whore, she was sad and swimming too.

— A woman receives the hopeless sorrow of a man between her loins. He can't bear it by himself.

— Seems the case. He's getting married this morning.

— Together cross that happy river.

A photographer from the East walked into the

charcoal. He was chewing tobacco and lugging a folded tripod.

— Philip Hine. Verisimilitude and illusionism is my game. I hear something is up. You'd be doing the sheriffing here?

— Har. Eh.

— Give me a chance, fellows. I'm broke.

— You dressed more western than anybody here.

— Like to blend in. This is a town of how many souls?

— Four hundred. Or that and forty if you count the hogs and Chinee.

★

Reverend McCorkindale looked at the cornet player and the pianist. The music was thin, a sort of sacred rumor of retreat. Both of the musicians were alcoholic, like almost everybody else in town. The whole American West, McCorkindale reflected, might be drunken eruption and hangover. He himself was drunk and horrified. Fernando was drunk and horrified. Nermer was conked on opium, he and the lesbian with him. Python Weems was drinking even now in the rear of the church. The two Chinese at the door with Spencer repeaters, who knew? They came out of such smoke and distress. Fernando had promised them the hotel.

Perhaps only Stella was full sober, and the preacher noted she looked better than ever in her life. In fact, as he married them, McCorkindale made a sort of pass at her, shocking himself so that his knee buckled and he dipped, then up again, smiling grimly.

— . . . tender ministrations in an existence too often nasty, brutish and short, he continued.

Python Weems disappeared to the airplane, looking neither left nor right.

The wedding party came out on the church steps, led by Fernando and Stella, a beacon in her rose dress with the morning sun straight on her.

— Very well my imp, said Luther Nix one hundred fifty yards down the street. He was off his horse now, and looked at Smoot kneeling in the road with his long Creedmore out front. Smoot seemed to be asleep on the thing — Occasionally I prefer the sanitation of a long-ranger, said Nix.

The weapon made a long startling *hoooom!* and flew up, but Smoot retained it, sitting flat on his haunches. On the church steps the woman in rose reeled back, disappearing into the dark slot of the door.

— The wrong mark. But hello, said Nix calmly. The other hirelings spread out into the town. The citizenry scattered at the noise and scuttled here and there for a safer view. More people than usual were about, combed out of the county by rumors. Main Street was clear except for the town idiot, who stood straight up near the Chinese shanties, taking a frank look about and discussing it with the hogs, who had looked up from the ruts.

Philip Hine, the photographer, dashed for the church and had just entered when he was knocked back by Reverend McCorkindale, who ran from the church in the direction of the river. Nix could hear Fernando or somebody howling now. The church steps were bare. Nix walked straight at the church, Smoot wobbling alongside with both the Creedmore and Snuffy's ten-gauge.

They were delayed by the yellow Winton Flyer turning into Main Street. Old Remington's conscience had attacked him and he wanted to stop the hostilities. A woman was driving the auto — Nandina, wearing goggles and a bandana over her hair like a Haitian woman. The ruts were narrow and crisp and the auto went down so that the passengers were at head level to Nix when the thing stopped in front of him. He and the dwarf were on higher ground. The dwarf was looking straight-on at the grille.

It was all an unnecessary dream to Nix. The old captain stood up in the car in an old white diplomatic suit run about with filigree. Nix was impressed by neither the uniform nor the automobile. Another burst of irrelevance was the handsome quiet black and white monkey leaping from the seat behind onto Remington's shoulder. The monkey and the man stared at each other with no interest for a moment. Nix had never seen a monkey but he gave it no more study than he would have an insect. Smoot could see the captain and the monkey above the windshield. The old lump came in his throat.

— You, sir. I'm requesting the offices of Judge Nitburg.

— He ain't here yet and there's his offices. Nix flicked his eyes over at the great heap of charcoal and the far cage of the jail. — In fact we're doing some arsonist-hunting right now, if your commodoreship don't mind.

— I have certain documents of interest. I'm surrendering . . .

— Like to see me miss from here, said the dwarf. He raised the ten-gauge and blew off Remington's forearm, the one that was waving the papers, the one that was away from the monkey. Shreds of blood, flesh, bone and paper flew fifty feet beyond the automobile. Nix had jumped to the side. Nandina stood in the car and shrieked down at the dwarf, whom she had never seen.

— Damn deafened me, Smoot! Nix raged at him. But he changed face. — I like you anyhow. You going to retire me. Go back to smoking cigarettes and being bored. Shut up, he called at Nandina. — We got bridegroom business.

They walked around the car and bleeding, quiet Remington, half out of the car with his head in mud.

— For our kind, the die is cast, said Smoot.

They were about even with the shanties, closing in on the church, when they turned to a racket behind them. Nandina had turned the car around and it was wallowing toward them without a grip for good speed yet.

— Why don't you put a slug from that howitzer in that grille there, Smoot?

— I can't. Not the car.

— Well I can. Give me the piece. Nix reached down just as the automobile got purchase and lurched fast at them, thirty yards or so away. Nandina got the vehicle to twenty miles per hour, and was bearing on them. But there was a spatting, just a spatting, noise from out front of the hardware store, smoke puffing out from the boardwalk. Nandina fell over and then a rain of heavier slugs popped the car from heavier guns at the mouth of the saloon. The car stopped and rocked. Nix narrowed his eyes. The sun was in them.

Four men were lifting their rifles, one his pistol.

— Got you covered, Mister Nix! shouted out one of the hirelings, maybe Rupert, the man of all wars.

Nix looked grim. — Perfect scum.

— That's the judge's daughter, Mister Nix, said Smoot. He seemed very sick.

— Wasn't any war required. Count those men, Smoot.

— Sir?

— You're counting the dead. C'mon, boys! C'mon down here with us! he yelled suddenly. Good work! Bravely committed!

— You're going to kill them all?

★

The biplane came over the street, leaving town with a pecking disregard for the earthlings, Weems and McCorkindale peering down as it banked and went *peckapeckapeckapecka*. The craft shadowed Nix and

123

Smoot, and the dwarf did not like it, not even for the quick second of blacked-out sun. That thing had been around during the fire.

— We got the navy, the air force, dead women. Shit, let's have foreign too, said Nix.

There was a Chinaman with a rifle at the door of the church. Nix reached, drew, fired at him negligently, and missed. The Chinaman went back inside.

— Come here, oh my angels! Nix shouted at the men. — Prayer meeting! The die is cast! Gawd, you're a skit, harfed Nix to Smoot. — I sure like you. The die is cast!

The tall and strong lesbian prostitute who got opium for Nermer had guided him around back of the livery stable and found the back door of the hardware store some minutes before. Nermer crouched terrified behind the counter, looking square into the face of the store owner, who was shutting his eyes, because there was loud shooting suddenly on the boardwalk just outside. Opium was bursting out of Nermer in big drops that fell on the oiled floor. He had a gun in his belt but he had not even thought about it. Tall Jane, in her high heels and blue wedding smock, came back from the door where she had watched the shooting. She squatted down, running her hand into Nermer's crotch, pulled on his manliness briefly, that wasn't it, and finally plucked out the gun. Then Tall Jane smacked hard on the wood with her high heels and walked out between the shooters and their dangling Winchesters. One was Rupert, man of all wars. The other was Tim Room, contemporary of Gabby's and a veteran old woman-shooter from the Indian campaigns. They were gazing at their hand-iwork in the Winton Flyer and hearkening to the boom of Nix up at the church. Tall and plain Jane, with a million abandoned male grunts in her ears, faced right and shot one in the ear, then turned left and shot the other in the ear. They fell spewing from the head as if cut down from wires.

She clattered back in, handed the gun back to Nermer.

— They killed two of my domino partners, she said, white-faced but not alarmed.

— Why you . . . , began Nermer, creeping up.

— I ain't even started yet. Light me those lan-terns.

— But . . .

— It's you that liked fire so much.

— Not in this place, pleaded the owner.

— The place come to me.

The woman walked out on the boardwalk and dashed a lantern on the head of each body, which lit up amazingly black and yellow. Then she took off her shoes and danced back and forth over the bodies and the flames, in and out and sometimes leaping very high.

— What the . . . ? Nix was viewing it all from fifty yards.

So was Smoot. — Hadn't ought one of us to shoot her?

— Still, Smoot, be still. He was smiling. Was he making the motions of applause with his hands? — You don't argue with art, man.

Then he seemed sad as the remainder of the hirelings gathered around him, looking over their shoulders at the flames and the harlot with the raised dress, yellow stockings.

— Fact, I've got in a rut here, dog it. Get in the church door, Gabby. You're special. I'm letting you.

— But I . . .

— I said *special*! he howled.

Was he going to cry? wondered Smoot. Or kill?

Luther Nix kicked Gabby viciously in the pants. The thin old man did a crippled length of aiming and headed to the church steps, holding his butt.

In the church the Chinaman, tallest of all of them and named Lin Hsu — though Fernando knew none of their names — walked away from the splatter of the bullet in the door, hurried down the aisle, and knelt. He said something. Fernando could not comprehend. But the man, with a scared, gentle face, repeated it and Stella, who knew a little from the maids, opened her mouth. Nothing came out for a minute, with Fernando holding her there behind the lectern.

— Well I'm kilt but I'm sorry for you. She's a fine gal and I'm thinking bad thoughts, Nando. But don't let me be glad, that ain't right. They've shot Nandina for some reason.

— Don't talk, try to save . . .

— You ain't ever been shot. You don't know what. I imagined you have loved her intense and long, though you never touched her, so you swore.

Tears fell from her big tubercular eyes.

— I always had a kind of tender jealousy of her. Why me and you ain't natural, she was the natural. I got the old knife scar from that rough man in Baton Rouge. It ain't looking too bad, is it?

Fernando shook his head.

— I had the grim lungs. For a while I had a envy bordering on insanity, wishing that elegant bitch would get older faster like the Cajun girls in south Louisiana, but Nandina would not oblige. She taught the school and she rode into town with her legs covered by her dogs, nipping at her fine sorrel. She'd gone to Miss Winnie's Finishing School in Galveston for the whole course. How she held herself. She had a genteel snoot to her, them flushed white cheeks after she rode, and she spanked that dust from her calves so fine with her hat. She *dressed* so well, darn it, and you was in thrall, I seen it.

— Nah . . .

— Shush it, my darlin' husband. I seen your imagination like a flickered magic lantern on a white sheet. I dreamt she was holding you in with a extr'ordinary number of arms and legs.

From her poor lungs Stella spat a line of blood and sputum bright on her rose dress.

— They've shot her and I'm still jealous, God forgive me. But tender jealous, I swear. The minis-

127

ter he said *tender,* dear Fernando. Darn it, I was something just for a little bitty short while and now I am dead, forgive me. I wanted her black hair.

— And all my fault. I'm dreadfuller than nothin, I . . .

Then he saw that she was dead.

Fernando looked up at a white man bending over the lectern with a camera in his hand. The man was looking at his new Quaker wedding hat.

— Are you a hired killer?

— No, sir. Philip Hine. A kindly verisimilitudinist. I believe I am witnessing a quite mournful actionist, Mister Fernando Muré. The hat threw me for a few minutes.

— You better git.

When Gabby leapt in the door mournfully, already shooting, the photographer ran wide, and then high. He did not stop until he was in the belfry house itself.

There was a great amount of gunfire in the church beneath him.

There was quite a wait as Nix and the others looked on the doors. Then Gabby came stumbling out, next waddling and kneeling. There was blood all over his legs.

— Now by Jim I'm all shot up, it ain't fair! He sat on the steps and began throwing his boots off.

— You look done for, Gab, said Nix, stepping up.

Old Gabby came down from his luckless rage and quietened like a sucking infant, hopeless bright

128

blue scout's eyes fetched up from red sockets.

— It ain't so bad. Just the legs. And I bet I kilt the Chinaman. The Chinamen shot me first, then Muré popped up from behind that ... shit ... *preacher* thing at the front. Was in there with that dead woman.

— You're a goner, seems, darlin', said Nix. — Ain't a mighty scout like Gab a pathetic angel when he's all done for. Done rode out of history. Nix opened the flap of his coat and then did nothing. He just howled, that roaring prolonged giggle again that touched a man in the last chamber of the heart. Acoustically, it was impossible, lapping both sexes.

— I'll do her then. You boys cover me. Ho! Nix was on the steps in one leap, then through the door with drawn gun. They heard a few bootsteps and then a long quiet.

— How good was Muré? the bald man with lugubrious mustache asked Gabby.

— Wasn't so much good as all over the place. Something, I don't know. He should have shot me dead.

— That wouldn't be him there, would it?

The men looked idly to the right window and there came a man charging around the side of the church toward the Chinese shanties. He wore a Quaker hat and he was gone through a fire in the door of one of them before hands ever hit a holster.

— That was a preacher, wasn't it?

— Naw. That was Muré, said Gabby.

All of them pronounced it Mur*ee*, as did all Fernando's world except for his uncle, who was at the Winton Flyer now, in shock and touching the corpse of Nandina with his remaining hand. He was crooning something about not being able to swim, and it spooked the hirelings on the steps.

— Look who's up and about, Stump.

— Gives me the geechies.

Smoot was at the door, calling in.

— He's not here, Mister Nix! He's run to the shanties!

— I know he ain't here. Bring 'em all in. Man's a rabbit. We got something wondrous on our hands.

The hirelings filed by Gabby, sitting on the steps. They looked right and left, the five of them remaining, vigilant to the point of idiocy. Up on the dais, Nix was kneeling over the body of Stella. He was pulling at her dress, gently and fastidiously, like some solemn priss in the window of Nell's finery.

— Oh, darlin' Missus Muré, my old army doggies is so tired, my old cavalry jacket so out of fashion, darlin' seraph. I been running for things, you know, I know you're listening, and I'm ready for things to run to *me*. These old tired feets. Look at them tender feet on her, Smoot. Look what you shot.

Nix had undressed the woman and flung the gown out to the side. Then he removed his filthy blue jacket, blood gone brown at the cuffs.

Smoot and the rest could barely be amazed by him anymore. He was going to possess the woman right in front of them. Right in the middle of pursuit, Fernando in the shanties and where else by now? They gathered close, however, though most looked back at the pews. Smoot, only Smoot, was able to cast himself into a zone of pure religious trance. It mattered and it did not matter, and both of the situations were enormous.

— There now. Let's be handing over that dear long Creedmore, Smoot.

— Sir?

— The lofty device, great little man.

— Sure, well. He handed the cruel rifle over to Nix.

Nix had already got the head off the woman and now he lifted it up, streaming, and rammed it neck-down on the muzzle of the Creedmore.

— Hold this. Don't let it fall for nothing, he told Smoot. Nix reached down and picked up the dress, knocking his hat back so the string caught his neck. Then he pulled the dress over his head and was suddenly wearing it, with bare white hairy arms and sunbrowned hands. The rose garment glowed, almost laughed you might say, under his dark jowls when his head popped out. He spat out his pipe and didn't even look where it fell.

— I ain't *in* this, the man with sad mustaches blurted before he thought. The dress was over Nix's gun and knife, but the men still hung there frozen.

But Nix was mild. A staggeringly mild comment came from his mouth.

— Maybe you weren't even invited, Cousin Smut.

Nix walked off the dais and up the aisle and out of the church without another gesture, holding the Creedmore with the head of Stella on it, her pale red hair wet around the barrel and her eyes closed.

— Imagine where he *is*? said Smut of the sad mustaches. — Shit, let's revolt. Fuck, or just hide.

— Can't you . . . *locate* a act of genius? rebuked Smoot. — Mister Nix has gone to smoke out Fernando Muré.

They heard Nix beginning to howl outdoors.

★

A man stepped through the men on fire outside the hardware store. He was an Indian, no doubt of that. They never found out who he was attached to. He stepped right through the fire, hair long and silver but with a Rough Rider hat on, and deerskin holsters for two pistols turned hammer-in at his navel. He looked at Tall Jane, then at the grieving owner, then Nermer.

— Not you, he said to Tall Jane. — *You.*

He was very old but he had spring to him.

Nermer ducked back behind the counter and pitched himself out the back door. He flung himself around to the alley, broke out into the main street, went down the alley east of the hotel, and panted into the backyard at the end of the railroad spur. There was no real cover but a tree with an unlucky man in it. A great fat coward unrewarded in life, a dealer in hams and sawdust, he had arrived on a buckboard unwittingly into crashing gunfire on the main street. He had whipped his horse around, spilling hams and sawdust, only to arrive under the tree, where he kicked away and strove up perfectly high among the branches, so he thought, to escape harm. But the Indian behind Nermer came up in the alley and let go one shot, almost by way of cleaning his action. The bullet struck the poor man through the hand. He fell down from the tree and broke his neck, right in the tough roots around Nermer. Everything was awful. Nermer had quick and thorough pity for the man, but he rolled behind his corpse. Eventually he owed him damned near everything. He could see smoke run in front of the sun and here came the Indian, who took to the rear steps of the hotel kitchen when he saw Nermer's gun. He was on the porch, really without much haste now, and began shooting down at Nermer.

Nermer sorely missed the cave and his animal family. The convivial magpies. He thought of Nandina, too, and her thrown-out schoolteacher's body, the hot galaxy of sperm he had urged into her, helpless as surf. Something popped the heel of his boot and he thought almost with unwanted largess of the imagination about Nandina, already powerful in death. He thought of the smoky parlors of sin, delicious idleness, the click of the pool balls and the most violent blasphemies over nothing at all. The great sweet warm wrath of climax in Nandina, again. She was a world, a whole merry dangerous gasping planet, and he had traveled her like a pilgrim, clouds trailing behind him. But he had been sapped entirely, naught remaining to the backbone hardly. Up the mountain without another choice, that was it.

There was an angry gathering of bullets into the corpse of the innocent bystander. This Indian was very mean. A slug passed through the toe of his boot this time. Why was he, Nermer, so necessary to someone? Why so ruthlessly after him? He turned over, prone, and spied past the dead man's hair. The Indian was busy reloading. But who *was* the man? How could he find such lone vendetta in this confusion?

It was a person grim as a surgeon over the task of reloading here on the rear stoop of the hotel, just standing there straddle-legged and it seemed now almost sleepily. The long silver hair of him, the narrow bleak face? Some burnt leftover, tougher than the desert, not even friends to himself? Nermer fired at the man, some sixty yards away, making no impression at all. The man did not even budge and blew a tight quad of lead at him, followed by a more careful blast that near tore the head off the unfortunate climber and made Nermer scoot back. Nermer was spattered and cried out against God.

Then he remembered the Indian child, the one he had shot in the desert years ago, simply because he had a new gun. He was overtaken by a vision of despair and vengeance. A grown Indian corpse was firing at him, plucked out of that desert and time, gripped down on the stoop, blowing hell out of him patiently — else the man made no sense. Nermer was a mere chicken, a yellow belly. There were plenty others to shoot. Nermer's animal and bird friends shrieked and took leave of his soul. The Indian would have him and he would be correctly in hell. Yet he fired once again, hiding behind the brains of the climber. It seemed something afflicted his pistol. He was positive he saw the bullet loop out and bump on the stoop railing. This horrid miracle brought tears of awe that seemed to flow *inside* his face.

The Indian was not even annoyed.

Then two Chinese came out on the stoop with rifles and shot the Indian in the back several times. They had been in the kitchen. The battle had been so curious it had taken them a full minute to choose sides. Finally they noted Nermer's singular abjectness and recognized the Fool of the Mountain. Also the Chinese boys were formally occupying the hotel, as per Fernando's promise. They were, too, slightly racist. They looked away with scorn when two negroes ran out of the alley and began raiding the corpse for cigarettes.

Nermer stood and realized that he had been hit four or five times by slugs passing through the body of the climber. Some of the bullets were hanging out of him half entered in sucking craters of flesh. They rattled off him when he shook himself. It was a miracle from Satan himself and it sickened him.

This was too much sin. He had not meant to return this far, this deep.

He had wanted only an enormous fire.

★

This particular affair had transpired just yards outside the window of Doc Fingo's office, where he had locked himself when the first report of gunfire was heard. Really it did not seem to matter much, for he was heavy onto the opium pipe with a little nick of morphine in the wrist vein too. Obed Woods was locked in with him. Woods was blackmailing him for three monstrous square meals a day in the hotel kitchen lately. His mode was not subtle. He promised to stand in front of the office and scream that Fingo was a queer if he was not elaborately nourished. They were table partners, in fact, and Fingo did not find this disagreeable. The town could see the man that Fingo had brought off morphine. It gave substance to his trade. He thought the Woods boy was striving, even, to act more politely all the time. He was not ungrateful and Fingo sometimes gave him money. Woods sat on the floor and stared at him, flinching with each shot down the street, then holding his ears and raising his eyes as the Indian on the stoop let off nearly right by them. The doctor sat down on the floor as well. It seemed the thing to do, though nothing was really that urgent. He went under his desk and dwelled on the pipe, long streams of sweet smoke fleeing to the ceiling. There was a nice soft kick in the back of his brain. A ricochet from Nermer broke the window and whacked the wall. Fingo was taken by pleasant inner visions of manly gunfire outdoors, the crackling and the booms. War has its romance, too, he mused. Rather cozy here, as men burst back and forth at each other, snapping metal. He heard something like a salvo just feet away. He was there, in the manly world of men and armed conflict! He pushed a finger above the desk top as a wistful target, feeling he was full in the fray, actually leading a sort of opiated assault on the army of his own shame. He was in it, he was off into it! He had a sort of cavalry in his ears, his own craven blood pouting away. Fingo once mended a broken dog and dwelled with the heroism of that act. Now the main fight seemed to be down the street, mooting away until there was an awesome boom and clattering of lumber. But all he could see when he looked out the front window was old Remington ranting away. The poor fellow seemed to have thrown his own arm off, looking for it down the street. Fingo looked back at Woods, still squatting, chubby and healthy on the floor.

— Chee. Somebody brought in da thunder!

★

The airplane, *peckapeckapecka*, made them look up again. The hirelings were all around the church door above Gabby, who still sat on the steps nursing himself. Smoot was out in the street, lagging a bit behind Luther Nix, who was ranting at the shanties.

137

Three Chinamen with rifles stood at one shanty door now, beholding the man in the dress.

Smoot did not care for the airplane. They did not need all this visiting. The street was not right either. Old Navy Remington, though silenced by the vision of Nix and the horror of the Creedmore, stood by the Winton Flyer as if it were still his, the monkey cuddled by his good arm, as if it were still his. The town idiot had not moved from the swine ruts, and he was glaring down. Some other officious fool was poking out of the door of the billiard room. You should not have these gawkers just standing around during your high adventure. Neither did Luther Nix like the plane. The rose dress flicked up behind, his Colt was out, and he banged away at it as it came low up the street, shadow in front again. He moved the Creedmore up and down, bawling, as the plane disappeared over the top of the church. You can't have tourists about. This thing was beyond and they would never know, even when they thought they saw.

The hirelings did not like the plane either. They backed farther into the church with a few imprecations.

What they saw from fifty feet above in the airplane was ghastly, and McCorkindale, who was piloting, had an instant, terrible sickness, and barely got them over the steeple and belfry.

Luther Nix walked forward to the Chinese, shaking the Creedmore and the head and railing for

Fernando. Then he changed into a little woman's voice, pumping the head more gently.

— Come out, dear Fernando, my husband. We never seem to talk anymore! Har!

Nix raised his gun and blew down one of the Chinamen.

So sudden, thought Smoot. The dress had them going like a cobra in a basket.

— Damned coolies, will you!? Shoot me, shoot me! Here I am, shoot me!

One man adjusted his rifle up and Nix walked right at him. He shot the man in the throat from fifteen feet. But the other man had raised his rifle too and got off a blast. How could he miss? Nix hurled himself toward Smoot. The right side of his face was bleeding. But he was laughing. Resumed roaring. He was beyond rifle lead, reckoned Smoot.

— Give me that, darlin', shouted Nix.

He ran a brief way and snatched the rifle from the man's hands. The man stumbled and ran back into the tarpaulin shanty. You could see where he bumped the sides of the canvas as he crawled inside it to another hovel connected behind.

— Yellow Fernando and your yellow men! Give me some more, I tell you! Hiding there behind them! Shame! Yellow, yellow!

Nix reached down and seemed to pick up the whole cooking fire at the mouth of the tent. He hurled it onto the roof and the tarpaulin went up instantly.

This time the plane came right over the hotel and the shanties themselves. Nix never looked up.

— Say now? screamed McCorkindale forward to Python Weems.

A sort of pipe tumbled out of the air right over the head of Smoot, fluttered into the church door and broke on the first pew beside Smut and Griffer, who had never uttered one word. The whole church went up, forward, backward, left and right, and straight up. Some of the splinters nicked the bottom of the Sopwith Camel. McCorkindale turned and saw the rest of the building collapse in upon itself.

— What? McCorkindale screamed forward, mean-eyed in his goggles.

Python Weems had called something back.

— Said you got a show all right, but it was really designed for your high troop concentration!

— All right!

Weems said something else. McCorkindale lifted his ear flap.

— Did you see that man in that steeple? shouted Weems.

Gabby was blown out into the street and woke riddled with splinters. The blast had flattened Smoot, too, and he was deaf, so that he heard no more of Nix's shouts and could only watch the quick and vast progress of the fire over the roofs of the shanties. He saw Nix go into the fire and become a part of it as it tired in the first hovels. The rose dress might be on fire, too. He was knocking greatly back and forth, clearing the way of flaming tarp and householdery. Then he went in deeper where the fire burned hottest. Even out here it was withering.

Fernando was on his knees behind a Chinese boy wrapped in a blanket. He himself was now on fire. The roof had flapped down on him and his black wedding suit began burning. His hat took up like a torch, and he cast it away, pounding his smoking head. Then the sawdust was on fire under him, agonizing his knees. A strut fell down and sat evilly right on his cheek.

Luther Nix came in the area thrashing and hollering. The head of Stella smoldered on the rifle, but he dropped it when he saw the wrapped child before his knees. Smoke and tatters had fouled his eyes and he looked again.

— Eh? said Nix.

Fernando shoved the child to the side and shot Nix four times in the stomach.

When Smoot saw Nix walk out of the smoke, the dress was burned off him and he was in only the pieces of a blackened undershirt. He did not look too interested in anything anymore. Then Smoot noticed he was punctured, not walking well, and bloody at the mouth.

Fernando came out some yards behind him. He was a burned wreck too, with an urchin in a blanket stepping behind him where it wasn't hot.

— Is it over then? I'm burnt up bad, said Fernando.

Nix sat down in the splinters and lumber around Gabby. Smoot had regained some hearing. Nix and Gabby seemed to be having some sorrowful conversation.

The dwarf stood beside Nix and knew he was going to die.

— Wasn't equal. There was a child. My angels, this should have been a neat little thing.

Nix glanced up dully at Fernando.

— Don't shoot me again. Give me a little more history here. Me and Gabby, bound for hell. His lips bubbled and Smoot finally surrendered, himself.

— Here's some history, Mister Nix, said Gabby.

Gabby had pulled out the great knife from Nix's sheath and fell on him, ramming long lengths of the blade repeatedly into Nix's liver. The old scout knew what he was doing. Nix screeched with each thrust. Smoot never thought he would hear this. But the man was still alive. He lay there, torn up and burned, but his eyes watched the sky and the dark sun, smoke flowing across it.

— Here's some more history, partner, said Gabby.

He began cutting Luther Nix's head off.

Fernando hobbled over and snatched the knife from him.

— Don't do that, old man.

Fernando was at the last of his strength. He almost toppled over. Then he raised up and stumbled toward the hotel and Fingo's office. His face, especially the right side of it, was pink-flaked and gruesome. He got a ways off before Edwin Smoot called to him.

— What about me? I'm a man!

Fernando returned, with pain and great loathing in his eyes, though there was now a change beyond despair. He sorted out the low Smoot from the lumber and blood and a kind of pity nestled on his features.

— That's always been a hard one for me, Smoot.

— Ain't I a killer? Ain't I shot down your . . . cunt? Ain't I blowed off your uncle's arm?

— Well. Fernando raised the gun without much determination.

— Not the gun. I want it like Mister Nix.

He was looking at the long knife in Fernando's hand.

— I ain't never been a knife man, Smoot. And I ain't got the strength.

— I'll shoot you where you stand, nigger! cried Smoot.

Fernando looked around again.

— Smoot, I'm not a nigger.

— In my world you are! You ain't never known my world! This ain't over! I'll shoot you where you stand!

Fernando turned again and came back, a last time.

— You probably would.

The pistol was out in his burned claw, but the

hammer fell on a spent round and clicked. The next one, live, splattered Smoot's heart. He was at peace before he hit the dirt.

★

L. P. Sheheen, often mistaken for a drunk, was the town fool who abhorred drink and kept a clean shirt on. He would enumerate with a curious zeal lacking in passion altogether a host of facts, a sort of history with the heart torn out of it. Neither by seeming will nor concern, he seemed to accumulate facts in a glut of the esophagus poured forth in an even vomitus knocked from him at a quarter to three every afternoon.

So he was yesterday's diary, like it or not, flat and unleavened for the most part, though the man tended toward Presbyterianism. Hardly a fact escaped him, this was the wonder, for he never seemed to be anywhere. Then he would float from some corner and his jaw would be going up and down: power, greed, lust, money, God, infamy, dust, ambition, death, the issues nicked off dead accurate and almost uninflected. He stood in the bullet-golden street the afternoon of the next day, babbling eastwardly, grim-jawed twenty-four-hour monitor, hogs circling him:

> — The sun was dark and hot. But their guns were long. There was no playing of billiards and no shouting, two days after our Lord's Birthday. The whores were in their whore rooms, quiet. Doctor Fingo was away, his hand on his smoke. You could

144

smell China over there. The piano was not playing. The church was not singing. The hogs, you hogs, did not know. The guns clicked and had eyes. The preacher was in the airplane with another man, who was a stranger. The yellow car of the sheep rancher sat tired at the horse trough, without smoke. The airplane was using the smoke now.

— The low man Smoot was there with those stranger-relatives. The courthouse was gone, flat black, with the airplane angry over it, cutting up the black wind. But you hogs walked back and forth and did not know. The bank said Bank and hid its money and the judge's morphine bottles over that great hole where folks threw their money down to, looking unhappy. Where they paid for dirt and rooves and their women would get bigger making more of them but not smiling about it, wishing the cactuses would do it for them. A woman will cry both ways, having it and having them. I know, though it is not for hogs' knowing, a woman's nook is so dreaded it makes a man holler and she's got to hang pretty cloth of all kind over her like a man don't need flowers nor lace over him. You see a woman she wears even a bonnet over her shameful face, bent over more for each child and looking at the ground talking to the Snake itself. The hole in the bottom of the bank, the hole in a woman, the hole right under us which is Hell of boiling reptile venoms and hairy fire, that is what is and that's always it no difference since God wrote out the world.

— Fernando fired the courthouse then went away and then the rough stranger-people, bought-en thwartness of aiming men come on the rail or coach or tuckered horse, not looking at the Bank with its great hole, but that was funny because the

Bank was the whole thing, my hog and sow children, suffer thy farrow too, the Bank, they walked just past it not even glancing at it like not glancing at your mother sitting in the middle of the room.

— But nobody hired the Indian. He came in seemed just for mean fun except it wasn't no smile on his face and he had the hair of something dry out there which had been blown in. He did not assort with no man. That colored quartet commenced singing and come out of the barbershop to trail him around like tall birds watching his fate but not quite knowing the words to it yet. He did not want them and he went away into fire and left them. The Indian had doeskin waders on and parched loins. He was the color of a dried-up hole of water in the desert. One of the colored quartet come up ask him what was the words to his fate and the old Indian look a hole through him come out the back of Amos's head and burnt up a child's pet lizard on the hitching rail.

— How it begun was not wrote out well for Fernando. We have callous disregard sometimes here in the West. Some say there was no glory in him or none of it at all, it was all ignominy and things simply gone that used to be there. They say was he hiding behind the Chinese child or was he saving the Chinese child. They say murder just a form of laziness extremed out. They say firing the courthouse was just rapid laziness. Say the airplane flying angry and concerned and the nitroglycerine had no glory in it either, just a unwelcome gnat over a frozen headache of a town where nobody couldn't get no grip on heroism nor even a cause. I was right near the old sheepherder without one arm when he yelled out I can't swim, I can't swim, you heard him too, oh my swine. There you heard, that was all it, a old man without one arm on the dry earth yelling I can't swim is what it all means, but you know and will never say, my hog listeners.

— The last to fall was the low man Smoot. He said to me once what he said to no other man. The salvation of a dwarf ain't available to regular earthlings, since he was low already and had a home in the roots where real things were. He could be near invisible where he stood, for most of the world chose not to look at him at all. So when he died he didn't go very far at all. And it would give his neck a wonderful rest from looking up. Some say there wasn't no glory in shooting a dwarf, neither. When the sun was not black no more and they could see, nobody minded much the others, but they hated to look at the body of the dwarf. Them as did look say he was pretty and pitiful and it made them cry.

— We will be here at the same time tomorrow, my children.

★

Agnes Dunning Nitburg sat beside her giant son Robert in his open buckboard with spring seats. The day was fresh and blue. Nandina's dogs ran a long way with them, then turned back, all the glorious eight of them, for water back at the manse. The automobile behind the buckboard had alarmed and interested them for a while, but they could not smell their mistress. Two Texas Rangers rode in the auto. One remarked again on the sad

147

death of Nandina. The dogs seemed lost and pathetic.

— And by the way, said the driver, — that old
woman doesn't even believe we're here. I mean,
she's got no credence in motored cars.

— A certain blindness ain't that bad out here.
What I say. *Keff. Hack.* The man speaking was a
crack shot, but a morbid whiner and hypochon-
driac allergic to Texas dust. He was red-nosed and
teary-eyed under the Stetson hat as the stuff came
in the windows. He claimed grandnephewship to
Kaiser Bill and deplored this barren plat in favor of
the Prussian woods and greens.

— Would you marry it? Wealthy blindness.

— Maybe if she'd cut her hair.

— She wants to worship.

— If she can find something left of the divine.

— Well it's all curious. We've got twelve bodies
and nobody's signed one paper yet.

— Maybe it's the last of something, said the
German. Your damned woolly West.

— Two things I think I'm really tired of. It hadn't
even barely started the century and every other
goddamned fool is going around saying *last.* The
last of this the last of that. And the other thing is
smart fucking krauts. Promise me you're the last
one. And give me the last of that whiskey. We're
looking at Volstead and the woman vote, Kaiser.

They watched the woman get out at the flattened
church. The steps were left but there was a great

hole in the floor and pews were blown away ten rows up. The giant son helped her up the steps. She went as far as he would let her with the cane, sunglasses gleaming in the morning sun, cracking the splinters with her high lace-up granny shoes. The church, blown at the mouth, retained its rear belly and main ribs. The steeple was still in the street, though some of its boards had been used for coffins. This did not involve the Chinese. Agnes Dunning Nitburg was on the gangway of a torn ark, is how it looked. Shredded hymnals and stacked pews were within her main grasp. Mc-Corkindale had been smoking cigarettes and tamping them out on the front pew, one of the few whole ones. She heard him move.

— Where is he?

— Me? asked the minister.

— I mean God. He still owes me and I want him.

— Mother Agnes, you're spared the sight.

— You seem to be in the air, young man.

— A murderer . . . standing in the filth of his own bomb.

— What's left, pastor?

— Maybe just that idiot in the street talking to pigs.

— Get God back in here immediately! I'm paying.

— Maybe folks aren't talking to God just yet.

— Then you . . . pretend, until he comes. I want music, I want the forms, I want the sad widows, I want the lustful minister, I want the hypocrites and the unpleasant children. All of it.

— You knew?

— Get blind long enough and you can smell it all, what you don't hear.

★

As for the judge, he never came back to town. But he didn't do much else either, except stare at the place on the picket fence where the head had been for a few months. He was not insane, Fingo figured. He could feed and clothe himself and make normal conversation. His wife said he was too mean to go insane, but the big son came and took her to live in the hotel. She delighted in dominoes with the "girls," pretending she did not know what the women were. They played badminton with her, too. She was a merry proprietor. Several of the sluts would attend church with her, and this was written up by a winking "local-color man" in the Austin newspaper.

Judge Nitburg still had a great deal of money.

But he told Fingo once that he could not think of one thing to buy.

Fernando Muré was a burned-scarred half-crippled recluse for two years at Navy Remington's ranch. He and the old man took care of each other, with the help of several Chinese.

The Chinese had not gotten the hotel and they followed him out to the ranch, haranguing him from outdoors day and night. Remington was

150

forced to put them to work as shepherds and kitchen workers. He gave them the barn. Things were fairly pleasant.

Philip Hine, the photographer, had lived through the fall of the steeple. He was explaining his point to Nermer and McCorkindale and Woods in the hotel dining room. Whispering, really, because Agnes Nitburg was sitting and reading braille barely twenty feet away.

— I'm a voyeur, you see, he said.

— You are? asked McCorkindale.

— Freely admitted. A peeping Tom. I'm speaking time and distance. Now really, what if a woman, say just an average sidewalk-walking woman, came in here right in your face, took off her clothes, I mean jaybird naked and just stood there with her things hanging out.

— Well. Not really so good, said McCorkindale.

— Offensive. Insane. Inappropriate.

— But, see, a woman at night across the way through gauze curtains, lighted from behind, doing the same thing with, say, just a little grace, just a little — here we are — slowness. See?

— Yeah. Must be one of dose meself. Voyoor, said Woods.

— Time and distance. Distance *from* the woman. The *time* it would take to *get* her. The whole thing becomes something else entirely. And who is to say not more real?

— So? asked Nermer.

— Fernando and all of you. It's been two years. Every day, more light from behind, more softness, more gauze. It's time we held the dance of history. You're all heroes, and folks will miss your kind. History won't let you hate yourselves anymore.

It was an agreeable theory and Philip Hine took it over to Fernando, fifty miles away. He was at the river fishing with Hsu, the Chinaman. His hair was full of silver now and his face was slack and grotesque on the right. He had a paunch. He walked painfully. His hands were black with worm dirt. He sat and listened to Hine courteously while the river lapped green and merry in the cove under the willows.

— None of that is right, Mister Hine, though thanks. You don't even seem to be wanting no money for it, either. Others has. *Have,* he corrected himself. — Thing is, it was all wrong and I am a villain. *Except.* I'm here studying up how I can make the next years fine ones, by my little Stella. I mean to be something extraordinary and make a high mark for good.

— But what will you do? Honestly your face . . . your looks, your whole legendary physical attributes. Well, forgive me, sir, but they're all *gone*.

— Yeah. Muré smiled, still with good teeth. — Maybe this time I'll have a whole lot better chance.